Strange Sands Suspense 4
Bluffton

The Dark Passage

Pamela Poole

I0544236

Southern Sky Publishing

Author's Note

Have you ever walked into a place and instantly became ill at ease? Did you ever meet a person and your spirit clashed with his or hers? Was there ever a time when you couldn't explain it, but you simply knew something bad might happen at any moment—and it did?

The novellas in the Strange Sands Suspense series will follow the adventures of a young lady named Mercedes Ellison, whose family has a long history of unexplainable encounters that many would call "strange." But then, Christians are peculiar people who should be living supernatural lives.

The stories and people in this series are fictional, but they are steeped in places I've been, situations I've experienced, and people I interviewed who have had a few of these encounters—encounters they typically keep to themselves. Each story will contain at least one of the events from my interviews.

I hope you'll enjoy the Southern Lowcountry ambiance in this series, where moments spent on warm sandy beaches blend with the grains of slipping sand in history's hourglass.

Chapter 1

"So, his heritage is 'landed gentry,' blended with an honorary line of 'Lord' so-and-so, and Knight so-and so. The assassin who spared him a few weeks ago at Majestic Oaks in Charleston said it was because of Quincy's family's long and distinguished service to England that he spared his life. Mercedes, you've known him since you were born, so why have you two never talked about his aristocratic background?"

Mercedes Ellison held her cellphone to her ear, huffed, and looked both ways before stepping off the curb to cross the street in the small town of Bluffton, South Carolina. "He never asked me to marry him before, Jana, and all that peerage and honorific titles stuff confuses me. Americans just don't think like that."

She reached the sidewalk to a popular local park and caught her breath. It was one of those Lowcountry mornings in August when the temperature was still bearable, but the air was like breathing in a sauna. Instinctively, she glanced around to be certain there were people nearby and nothing looked suspicious before she spoke on her phone again.

"Jana, I'm just trying to explain why I'm hesitating about planning a wedding. Quincy's grandparents hoped he'd marry a lady from a titled old British family. Then the entire world went upside down and people resented those titles, and Quincy and his dad left archaeology, changing their career plans and country of residence. His grandparents were already in upheaval, selling family properties or turning them into commercial ventures. That's why they came to live here."

Mercedes sighed and turned to watch children playing in an ingenious pirate ship built with slides and a gym. Some of them squealed in delight, ignoring the heat, their hair already plastered to their foreheads with sweat. Their laughter was contagious, and she grinned.

Jana sounded sympathetic. "I have heard that change is hard for older folks."

"If so, they're kind enough not to complain around me. Quincy followed his father's footsteps by becoming engaged to an American woman, so they are losing another generation of connections to the society they grew up in. It's crumbling anyway, but it must be unsettling for them. His grandparents are wonderful people, Jana. I don't mean to come across as if they are a problem. I want them to feel appreciated, and that's partly why I'm so conflicted about how to make our wedding something they will approve of, while still pleasing the American side of our families."

"Yeah, back in the day, their wedding was probably a society event. But you said Quincy's grandparents aren't the real problem. Then what is?"

Mercedes bit her lip, glanced around again, and raked her hand through her hair. "I don't want to be the reason Quincy leaves his heritage behind."

Jana groaned. "Oh, Mercedes! You aren't the reason! Listen, he made that decision before he moved here, before you got back together, before asking you to share his life with him. I mean, would it be so bad to be the 'Lady of the Lake' or whatever?"

Mercedes burst out laughing and her mounting tension dissipated. She turned to face the street, eyeing the house she planned to walk past when she set out. She had admired it ever since moving to her rented cottage for the summer. Something about the crisp red shutters against the white siding, the gracious deep porches with inviting wicker seating, and the uniquely carved trim moldings always turned her head.

Then she looked back to the park, where a child in a superhero cape conspired with another boy wearing a tee shirt sporting the same superhero. "This isn't a Regency novel, Jana. It's my life," she mused. "Titles come with responsibility and baggage.

A sudden shriek made her spin around, and what she saw made her heart jump. "Jana, did you hear that? I've gotta go—I'll call you back later."

Stuffing her phone in her pocket, Mercedes watched for traffic and then ran across the narrow street. An older woman stood grasping the railing on her veranda, looking stunned and sobbing hysterically. She had gray hair pulled back into a short ponytail, and she wore a loose cotton blouse over capris, but she had the look of another time and place.

Mercedes heard footsteps behind her as she rushed up the old wooden stairs. "Mary Lou," she gasped. "Mary Lou, what's wrong?"

Her eyes met the woman's wild gaze, then she glanced down to see a lean young man in sweaty jogging clothes arrive at the bottom stair. He claimed to be a doctor and breathlessly asked if he could help. A young lady wearing a bright yellow bandana arrived almost at the same time and stood looking up at them, introducing herself in a thick Southern accent as Tricia, an off-duty EMT.

But Mary Lou ignored them, gulping several times and keeping her hazel eyes locked on Mercedes, who saw her desperation and set the weight of her hand on the woman's thin shoulder to calm her. Then she said gently, "See, we're all here to help, Mary Lou. Tell us how."

"Inside—inside," Mary Lou blurted, and she began sobbing again. Brokenly, she said, "It's Doran, my brother—back in his studio!"

Mercedes' heart fell, and dread swept over her, but so did the adrenaline rush she would need to help this distraught neighbor. In an instant, she knew why the doctor and the EMT were providentially on the scene. "Is the studio door unlocked?"

The woman nodded, shuddering, putting her work-worn hands over her time-weathered face. Mercedes looked around at the waiting young doctor and the anxious EMT. With her free hand, she pointed toward the backyard. "We're so grateful you're both here! Something has happened to Mary Lou's brother, in the studio behind the main house. Go past a connecting passage to a garage-type building with skylights and a glass door. I'll join you in a few minutes, after I call my friend to stay with Mary Lou."

Mercedes' landlady and good friend Lois kept her distraught neighbor, Mary Lou, on the other end of her phone for the few minutes it would take her to arrive at her house. Mercedes hurried to join the doctor and Tricia and see if she could help.

The studio door was propped open, and as she hurried through it from the bright sunshine, she encountered the familiar smells of a place where art is created. There was a wafting scent of acrylic gesso. This was a relief, because it meant the artist used acrylics. Even with good ventilation, oil painting supplies gave her a raging headache.

Her eyes adjusted and she glanced around. The art space was enormous and mostly open, though head-high shelving partitioned off some sections. Research on the house had revealed that this studio had formerly served alternately as a garage and workshop.

Overhead, the drone of an annoying, faint buzzing sound made her pause. She looked up at the rafters, hoping it came from outdated fluorescent lighting or equipment. But she shivered, her instincts saying it was something else.

Something she had heard before.

Blank canvases leaned against a bare wooden wall, and shrink-wrapped large frames hung on racks. Warped, aging plywood shelves were paint-spattered and loaded with paint bottles and tubes, brushes, palette knives, water containers, towels, and other artist tools. Mysterious draping covered the artwork resting on half a dozen rickety, paint-stained wooden easels.

Except for one. It was apparently the artist's work in progress, because the doctor and Tricia had just found the artist on the concrete floor in front of it. Mercedes heard them stifle expressions of surprise and dismay, and she tore her eyes from the shocking painting to go see if she could help.

A nearby easel had crashed to the floor and lay broken. Red, yellow, and black paint were splashed and dried over the area. At least, she hoped the red splotches were indeed paint.

The doctor was checking for signs of life in a person on the floor—Doran? But the young EMT was staring at Doran's face.

Mercedes took a tentative step forward to have the same view, then gasped before clapping her hands to her mouth. Her knees felt weak, and she staggered a few steps back into the wall. She shuddered, wanting to drag her eyes away. But she could not.

Tricia came to stand in Mercedes' line of sight. She noticed how shaken Mercedes was and gently took her arm to lead her away. "There's nothing we can do for him now, honey," she said in a low voice. Compassion filled her coffee-brown eyes. "He's been gone for hours. Just stand over here while I call for help, okay now?"

"But—his face—" Mercedes rasped.

The young EMT sighed and glanced back at the body of the artist with a troubled look. "Yes. I know. It's a first for me, too."

While Tricia made a call to report what they had found and ask for help, the doctor came over. He nodded, a signal that he would keep Mercedes away from the disturbing sight of the body. The EMT wandered toward the open studio door, answering questions over the phone.

Mercedes wished the two medical pros would simply tell her to stay put. After all, she was not hysterical, and she understood the need to keep a distance in case this was a crime scene. If they knew what she had seen this summer, they would not treat her as if she were an impulsive child.

But they did not know, and she was glad. She meant to keep it that way.

Averting her eyes, she turned to the painting she saw earlier. The doctor noticed her interest. "That's not the work he's known for. I collected one of Marlowe's old paintings, a waterfall landscape, from a time when he explored Africa. A small one for him, but magnificent, painted on location and shipped back. I grew up spending summers here in Bluffton, and he was a legend among my friends. We kept up with local news about his dangerous adventures. Quite a character."

Mercedes cleared her throat, but her voice still sounded brittle in her ears. "Thank you for giving me that perspective about his life. What do you make of the painting he was working on last night?"

"It's a dark fantasy from a deeply troubled mind, and frankly, it unnerves me. A commission, perhaps. Any thoughts?"

She hesitated, studying the scene, wondering whether to be straightforward. Did he want her opinion about the painting, or was he trying to keep her distracted because a very dead man with a look of terror frozen on his face was only feet away?

It was tricky to talk to people she just met about her real thoughts. This doctor may have no spiritual beliefs, and this was no place for a discussion on invisible beings and realms or the existence of heaven and hell—or which destination the artist was currently living in for eternity.

Displayed on the easel was a depiction of two realities happening at once, both seen and unseen, earthly temporal, and endless spiritual time. The bottom was Dante-like, an infinite black abyss or underground tunnel where grotesque half-animal creatures tortured what must be human souls. The acts being committed were vile and unspeakable, so she quickly looked up instead. Humans were on land above, unaware of the hellish realm below their feet, bowing in worship before an altar where another human was being sacrificed. Blood was being collected into a goblet and it stained the altar, and a sky over the scene was blood-red. Behind the altar stood a massive statue of something like a chimera, part human, part animal, part male, part female, with chilling black, blank eyes.

But it was the being that was concealing itself behind the statue, through an open hole in an upright slab of rock, that made Mercedes' heart race. She knew it, yet she didn't. The hideous evil entity held a glowing round orb-like object, twirling a crooked claw-like finger over it as if controlling the minds and actions of the humans that bowed to the statue. Perhaps the artist was working on the being but didn't finish it because he was interrupted.

Mercedes jerked back to reality when flashing lights raced over the shadowy areas on the walls of the studio through the windows. She heard Tricia's velvety deep voice greeting law enforcement and handling their questions.

Knowing her time left in private with the doctor was short, Mercedes looked over at him. "Yes, I have some thoughts. The most important one is that I believe Doran Marlowe encountered the being he was portraying in the painting. And he never finished the image."

"The bruises are typical for a fall to the floor, perhaps even from stumbling over that overturned easel," reported the young doctor to an officer in the studio. He slipped his driver's license identification into the pocket of his running shorts. "But I've never heard of any natural cause of death in which the deceased had such an expression on his face. I suggest looking for a hallucinogen and running tests on anything he ate or drank from. The same goes for any candles, incense, or such things that may have been burning."

The officer jotted down notes and nodded. "Are you suggesting suicide or foul play, Dr. Kirk?" he asked brusquely.

The doctor hesitated, looking around again for clues and rubbing his neck. "Not necessarily. He may have picked up some substance in his international traveling days and just used too much by mistake. I'm an acquaintance of the deceased man and even collected one of his older paintings. I can tell you he feared nothing, and his life was an adrenaline rush. He used to be a guide to places in the world where none of us would go. If your team is on the way and the coroner doesn't mind a tag-a-long, I'd like to hear his opinion."

"And how did you come to be here today, sir?" asked the officer.

The doctor explained that he heard Mary Lou scream as he was jogging near the house. "I never jog with earphones in, don't believe in it," he continued. He pointed to Mercedes. "This young woman was on the scene first, comforting Marlowe's sister and trying to discover what was wrong. But we haven't met yet."

He smiled and stuck out his hand to shake hers. Mercedes offered her own and noticed his grip was firm and confident. He said, "I'm Jansen Kirk."

She gave him a slight smile and nodded. "Mercedes Ellison."

The officer's head jerked up from his notes and he studied her. "Did you say—you're *Mercedes Ellison*? Uh, I need some identification, please."

Mercedes exchanged a knowing look with him and fished in her shorts pocket. Her mouth went dry as she handed him her South Carolina driver's license. She resisted rolling her eyes as she thought, y*es, I'm Mercedes Ellison, and yes, through no design of my making, I'm in the middle of another bizarre mess this summer!*

After studying the information and photo on her license, the officer was much less formal than before. "Charleston is your home address," he stated, and his voice had an edge of excitement. He almost gushed as he introduced himself as Officer Cordero and asked her how she came to be in Bluffton at the Marlowe house.

"I've never met the deceased—uh, Mr. Marlowe, that is. I've only known his sister, Mary Lou, for a few weeks. We met through my work with a local historical society. I'm an architectural historian, and she contracted me for some required official paperwork to be filed before remodeling this house. It's true that I'm from Charleston, but I'm spending the summer in Bluffton, in a rented cottage just down the street from here. My landlady is with Mary Lou Marlowe right now, in the main house, if you'd like to check with her. She and Mary Lou know one another from years past."

Officer Cordero's dark head bobbed as he jotted down notes. Another law enforcement vehicle and an ambulance pulled into the wide sandy parking area, without sirens or flashing lights, so the officer excused himself to go meet them.

Mercedes turned to find the doctor staring at her. He wore a puzzled half-smile and said, "You must be famous for your name to perk up the ears of an officer of the law. Or is 'infamous' the right description?"

She sighed and rubbed her forehead, feeling suddenly weary. Sweat trickled down inside her shirt from the sweltering humidity that made the temperature in Bluffton feel like it was well over a hundred degrees.

"I've had an eventful summer," she replied. Then she looked back up at him. "Your name is recognizable as well. Are you descended from the historic local Kirk family, as in Kirk's Bluff, the Kirk homes that were burned during the Civil War, and the graves in the Zion cemetery near the Baynard mausoleum—the one with the upended torch consuming itself?"

The grin faded, and he blinked his surprise. "Yes. Distant relations—very distant. You really have done your homework about the area, Miss Ellison." Then he looked at her hands for rings. "Or is it Mrs.?"

"Miss, for now. I'm engaged."

"Dr. Kirk!" called a man in the driveway, and his badge flashed in the sunshine as he beckoned. The doctor nodded back, and Mercedes rushed to say, "Thanks for helping, and I hope someone can solve this mystery soon. I really have nothing else to offer, so I'll check on Mary Lou. Goodbye."

"Wait," Dr. Kirk blurted, putting out a hand to her but taking a step backward toward the waiting group. "Hey, can I see you again—to talk about that painting, and about what's happened? I'd like to check in on Doran's sister while you are with her."

Mercedes hesitated, then kept her tone noncommittal. "I plan to work here at the house if she wants to proceed with plans she and her brother made for the property. If you check on Mary Lou, you can send word to me through her. My friend Lois, or I will come over."

She turned toward the house, away from the flashing lights, curious bystanders along the road, and many voices around her buzzing with reports and speculations about the body found in the studio.

Her footsteps crunched on the sand and oyster shell driveway. It was oddly comforting, a grounding, familiar sound from her summer spent here in an earthy town bathed in sunshine.

Chapter 2

The closest entrance to the house from the parking area was through a door in a passageway that connected the main building to the studio. The crunching of shells underfoot slowed, then ended, as Mercedes studied it. For no reason she could explain, the passage repelled her.

The structure may have been a cheerful, airy place in the past, like an enclosed breezeway or porch. Someone covered the windows with drapery, and something was pushing the fabric against the glass in several places. Even if the passageway was air-conditioned, she imagined it to be stifling and gloomy inside. And at night, with no sliver of moonlight allowed through the windows, it would be darker than dark.

She tried to shake the strange feeling of menace directed toward her from the passage. There was no need to go through that door, for she would see its contents soon enough with Mary Lou. This odd situation could not have occurred to her when she researched the house and accepted the job.

Mercedes turned decisively to the main house, toward the steps leading up to the welcoming veranda that hugged the structure. The groomed hedges at the banister railing were in their summer glory and provided some waist-high privacy between the house and the pointed spikes of a black ironwork fence along the street. The wafting scent of mock orange calmed her, while bees hummed happily among the blooms.

"Excuse me, Miss Ellison!"

Mercedes recognized Officer Cordero's voice and heard his hurried steps on the driveway as he approached. She sighed before turning and kept her hand on the painted wood banister.

He was winded, but said, "I'm sorry to bother you, Miss Ellison, but can you tell me why you changed your mind a minute ago?"

With his pen poised over the notepad, the officer watched her face and waited. Blankly, she looked back at him, brows raised. "Changed my mind?"

"Yes. You knew the door nearest you would take you into the house. You also knew you could enter the studio and check on Miss Marlowe. But you considered them and then came around to the front door, which is a longer route."

Mercedes watched his eager brown eyes. He was fishing, she knew. But she had no desire to get involved in this investigation. Was he hoping she would expose another underground antiquity thief, uncover another bizarre Civil War era cold case murder, dig up another long-lost cache of treasure—or bring to light a sensational mystery that might help explain the expression on Doran Marlowe's face when he died?

Over his shoulder, she saw the doctor and two other men watching them, waiting for his report. Irritation washed over her, but she masked it with a benign smile.

"Officer Cordero, I wasn't aware that anyone was watching me, and I didn't mean to give anyone the impression that something sinister was going on. I left Mary Lou and my friend Lois in the front living room. It seems more respectful to return to the front and knock. I hope you and your team do the same when you go to question her and give her an update."

The officer pursed his lips, but his scowl and searching eyes gave way to a twinkle and a nod. "Oh, yes, of course. We will. We just thought—well, witnesses often don't mention something that turns out to be important. If you think of anything later, anything at all, I hope you'll use my card to contact me."

Mercedes held his eyes and assured him she would keep that in mind. "I didn't think of myself as a witness, officer. Is this a crime scene?"

He blew out a deep sigh and glanced at the ambulance. "Miss Ellison, that's unclear."

"I don't know what you're going to say to Mary Lou Marlowe about what happened to her brother, but if there's been foul play, I didn't see it, and I'm not qualified to collect and analyze evidence. If you need to call on me about what part I played today in discovering Doran's body, I will cooperate with authorities."

"I don't like this, Mercedes. You're not a psychic investigator. The police and detectives shouldn't be watching you for clues about what happened."

Mercedes winced at Quincy's curt statement. This wasn't the tone he used when talking to her, but she knew he was under stress from overworking at the archaeological site in St. Augustine, Florida. He had taken extra time on his lunch break to even return her call.

She changed ears for her phone and sagged into the tropical flowers on a poolside lounge chair near the French doors to her cottage. "And I don't like choosing my words carefully around authorities, veiling what I'm thinking and possibly casting suspicion on myself. I felt forced to hide something I know applies to the situation, but it's not acceptable as tangible evidence. Maybe there *is* a hallucinogen involved in Doran Marlowe's death, as the doctor suspects. You know, there were powerful concoctions used in pagan religious rituals. Doran traveled extensively and may have picked one up."

"Sure, they exist. But the doctor is throwing around ideas because he knows something doesn't fit. I like a good Sherlock Holmes mystery, but the doctor is limiting his thinking through the scientific lens he's comfortable with, not a spiritual one."

Mercedes gulped the humid Lowcountry air. Her heart was racing at the memory of what she saw that morning. "Yes, of course," she said in a small voice. "You're under a lot of pressure right now, and I'm sorry to bother you. But I knew you'd want to know what's going on. And you're the one who understands why I feel helpless that all I can do is watch this play out. That buzzing noise—"

"I'm coming back," he said decisively. "I'll tie up some loose ends here in the morning and tell the team I'll be working from Bluffton for a few days. Hopefully, I'll be home by dinner tomorrow, so let's go out to eat and talk about it. Is Mary Lou there? Maybe you should stay with her tonight. Or you could go home to Charleston for a few days. Have you called your parents about this?"

Mercedes turned to the main house. "I wanted to talk to you and get some clarity before I called them and told Zeke. Lois brought Mary Lou back to stay with her, probably for the week. Mary Lou is understandably distraught and shouldn't be alone. Some of Lois' church friends are here making dinner, and her pastor has been amazing, comforting Mary Lou and handling important arrangements about Doran. She's only been back in America for a few weeks and doesn't know where to go to handle these things."

The rustling sounds in the background told her Quincy was already preparing to leave camp. "There's nothing like a church family in times like this. So, Mary Lou still wants you and Lois to go back to the house with her tomorrow for the assessment so you can stay on schedule for the next job in Beaufort?"

"Yeah. But—I hope to talk her out of it."

She heard him snort softly. "Oh, yeah? Is that for her sake, or yours?"

Mercedes closed her eyes and laid her head back on the lounge chair. The longer Quincy talked, the more he sounded like himself. "I wish I'd never accepted this job, Quincy. Why didn't it feel like it wasn't right for me? I don't want to enter that passage or go back into that art studio. When I tell you specifically what Marlowe was working on, you will understand. But I'm also not willing to leave Mary Lou alone to deal with this."

The background sounds on his side of the phone ceased, and she knew she had his attention. "You told me what the doctor said to you about the painting. Are you feeling up to describing it to me, or do you want me to see it for myself?"

Despite the muggy heat of the late afternoon, Mercedes shivered. She rose from the palm-shaded lounge chair and strolled around the edge of the sparkling pool, letting the warm caress of the sun soothe her.

"Mercedes?"

She ran her hand through her blonde bangs, pulling them back. "I'm still here, just getting out into some sunshine." Haltingly, she explained what Doran Marlowe was painting at the time of his sudden death. When she tried to describe the being behind the stone portal and the idol, Quincy told her to stop.

"Don't, Mercedes. I'm sorry. I get it now. Don't dwell on the painting. I'm calling your brother, so you don't have to talk about it again for now. Can you sleep tonight?"

Mercedes nodded as if he could see her. "I might call you for a few minutes first."

"Of course. Mercedes, are the painting and the dark passage related, and are they relevant to Marlowe's death? Is that what you dread so much?"

She gulped, and her voice sounded strangled. "I hope it was my imagination, but there's a menacing presence in it. I've felt it before, at the dig site in Peru. How could it be here? As for the painting, after Dr. Kirk said it was from a troubled mind, he asked me for my thoughts. I told him—"

Her voice broke off, and she drew a shaky breath. "I said that I believe the artist encountered the being he painted, but I didn't tell him it's still in the studio. I heard it."

Quincy jogged out to the expansive canopy that shaded the dig site where he was working as an independent consultant. His heart pounded in his own ears, but not from his rush to find the archaeology team. He wiped sweat from his brow and replaced his Panama hat, explaining to the others that he had an emergency matter to handle back at his cottage. After he left by noon the next day, they could reach him by phone until he returned.

He saw the annoyance and frustration on some of their faces, but it did not matter. His role was research and networking, not the drudgery he had been helping with, sifting through the dig because unreliable workers decided not to show up.

He hoped the sponsor would fire him for leaving. It would not damage his resume.

Memories of other dig sites kept passing through his mind like slideshows, distracting him so much that he packed his suitcase instead of trying to focus on the paperwork at his desk. It felt like another lifetime ago when he had been a lead archaeologist or worked on his dad's team, encountering altars stained with blood, evidence of broken and burned bodies, skeletons of children sacrificed to pagan gods, bizarre, enshrined idols, and carved pictures or writing. And in one of those lifetimes ago, when they had worked on a site said to be a portal to another realm, Mercedes was there with the team. It had deeply affected her.

Quincy never feared those discoveries, but they sickened him. And the more he learned about the supernatural histories behind them, the more he shunned working on those sites. He preferred revealing the brighter side of humanity's accomplishments.

As he smoothed out some folded shirts, his tanned hand trembled against the crisp white fabric. He stood up straight, closed his eyes, and drew a deep breath while saying a silent, desperate prayer.

Quincy knew Mercedes sensed what she was up against, but he saw now that she was far over her head. For all his bravado about rushing back to be there, he may not be any help to her.

Lois's friends from church and the neighborhood worked quietly around her house, preparing meals for a week ahead and making phone calls to add Mary Lou to their prayer circle. Some calls were to the older adults in their church without computers for email or cell phone texting. The pastor's wife fussed over Mercedes as she came in, concerned about her state of mind and her nerves after witnessing the scene in Doran Marlowe's studio. They were ready to make up a room for her to stay in the house with Lois.

"I'm still a little shaken. But I think I'll be fine in my cottage tonight," she assured the ladies. She lingered in the kitchen to thank them, meet fresh faces, and enjoy the wonderful aromas of their efforts. They knew about Lois' kitchen list of Mercedes' food limitations and showed her some specially labeled dishes. Then they said she had time to visit with Mary Lou and Lois before dinner was on the table.

As Mercedes took quiet steps into the living room, she heard the pastor asking Mary Lou about her missionary work. Aaron, Lois's close friend, rose from his seat beside her and motioned for Mercedes to sit down. He waved a silent goodbye to Lois and the others, then whispered to Mercedes that he would see her the next day.

"Yes, there were many hardships, compared to the life I had here." Mary Lou's voice was hoarse as she answered the pastor. Her eyes were red rimmed and swollen from hours of crying, and she looked as if she had aged a decade. Mercedes tried not to show her surprise at Mary Lou's condition as she settled on the sofa. Mary Lou added, "Many nights I huddled to sleep, sometimes hungry, sick, and discouraged, ready for heaven. But it was no different for the others who served with me."

"Why did you stay?" asked the pastor.

Mary Lou turned to stare out the window, and just when it seemed she had not heard him, she spoke. "I believed Jesus called me to serve Him that way. I committed to doing my best wherever the opportunity led to share the Gospel. But by the time I retired and returned home, I wondered if I had misunderstood. People do, you know. We want something, so we think the Lord is leading us that direction."

With a long, ragged sigh, she turned forlorn eyes back to the pastor. "Our mission groups left tribes better off than we found them, by modern health standards. But after all that, the teams who came in to relieve us had few authentic Christian believers to train as disciples and help grow a church. Most people just added Jesus to their shelf of gods. I know the work wasn't mine to succeed in. I was only a seed planter. Any soul won was the Lord's work. Now that my time there is spent, I wonder if I wasted it."

A sob escaped her throat before she put a trembling, work-worn hand to her mouth and squeezed her eyes shut. Mercedes and Lois glanced at one another, but the pastor's eyes never left the distressed woman, and he held out a pretty tissue box with a sunlit pastoral scene.

When Mary Lou opened her eyes and fanned her flushed face, she reached gratefully for a soft tissue. The pastor returned the box to an end table between them while she took a deep breath. "So, after spending my life sharing about Jesus in places that He seemed to have forsaken, I've returned to a pagan country that's no better spiritually than unreached people. Worse, in fact. At least the tribes had some rules."

The pastor could not stifle a snort before it escaped. He grinned and said he might use her point in Sunday's sermon, which prompted a small smile from her.

"Of course," she said. "Under better circumstances, we can talk more about those years. Lately, someone has been on my mind for no apparent reason. When I met him, he was a teenager, in South America, one son of what Americans would think of as—I believe you say, a witch doctor, or shaman. I get confused sometimes, switching my mind back and forth from that language. This young man's name was hard for me to understand because it was based on a god that I did not know. Like Daniel and his friends in the Bible, who were renamed for the Babylonian gods."

Mary Lou relaxed and sank back into the cushions of Lois' living room chair. "This young man, he faced strong resistance from his father when he believed in Jesus as his soul's Savior. He was hungry to learn the Bible. He knew Jesus was real, not only because creation proclaims Him, but because he said he and his mother had seen Him in their dreams. Other spirits warned the tribe not to listen if He came to your dreams and visions. When we baptized him, the young man asked us to rename him John, to honor John the Baptist, who prepared the way for Jesus. By the time another team of missionaries arrived, he was one of only a few true believers."

Mercedes leaned forward, clasping her hands together. "Mary Lou, when this young man comes to mind, what is he doing?"

The pastor looked startled. Mary Lou said, "This will sound silly to Americans who expect a natural explanation for everything. But, when I think of John these past few days, he wants to tell me something. He was so inquisitive back then, but he loved to share information to help us."

Her mouth twisted, trying to fight a grin, and she chuckled to herself. "The people there, they found my name difficult. So, they just called me Lulu. The children, they loved to say it!"

Then she sobered, looking into Mercedes' eyes. "When I remember John lately, he is saying, 'Lulu, I know a thing. I will help.'"

Quincy adjusted a setting on the camper air conditioner and said, "Can you take Aaron or Lois' pastor with you to the house tomorrow afternoon? I'd feel better if you three ladies weren't alone."

He plumped his musty pillow and settled into his camper trailer bed on the dig site in St. Augustine, Florida. A sense of foreboding haunted him, and he could not get his fiancée's ordeal out of his mind. Finding a dead body wasn't something that happened every day, so he called to check on her.

Mercedes turned the covers back on her bed. "So, would you feel better if we called Ghostbusters or something?" she teased.

"No, they're too old for this kind of work now."

"Good point. The pastor is taking Mary Lou and Lois to make funeral arrangements in the morning. Then, I'm eating lunch with them. Aaron is helping a contractor friend with a remodeling client, so I'm uncertain what time he will be available. I'll try to relax here in my cottage and finish a painting in the morning."

"Hmm, I like the sound of that. Painting, I mean, not ghost hunters. Sometimes I wish you didn't have a career, that you'd just follow me around to dig sites and museums. But then I remember there's no safe place. A calling follows a Christian wherever we serve."

Mercedes turned off her bedside lamp and sank back into her pillow, appreciating the faint scent of a coastal breeze in the laundered pillowcase. "Callings are sticky things when we tell Jesus we'll follow His plan. I seriously tried to find a safe place, though, remember? I chose a career characterized by lots of boring paperwork and stuffy archives. Look where that got me!"

"Yeah. I get it. My dream career didn't work out, either. But the Lord chose a new direction for me, and I'm much happier with you."

"Quincy?"

He drew a contented sigh, as if expecting dreams of pleasant things. "Mm-hmm?"

She bit her lower lip, then replied, "Oh—nothing. You sound worn out. I'm sorry this has interrupted your job, but I miss you and I'm glad I'll be seeing you tomorrow. I'm grateful that you can face this with me and keep me steady."

His voice was drowsy. "Me, too. You'll sleep okay then? No jitters?"

"I hope so. Being around everyone at Lois' house calmed me a lot, and all the prayers covering this place feel like a blanket of peace. It helps to know I'm not alone. Maybe I jumped to the wrong conclusion—I don't know. I'm tired and it all seems far away now."

Quincy yawned, then said, "I'll keep my phone right here if you wake up and need to talk. This is another road in life that we'll travel together, so sleep well. I love you, Mercedes, and I always will."

Chapter 3

Thunder and lightning sometimes roused Mercedes from a deep, luxurious sleep during the night. She loved summer storms. The flashes of lightning and the trembling cottage walls did not disturb her.

With a quick prayer before sliding back into slumber, she expressed her gratitude for the shelter and peace inside. She pushed aside all the looming challenges in her life. They were better dealt with in sunlight.

It was perfect weather for sleeping in. When the rumble and boom of thunder finally awakened Mercedes, it interrupted her dream of a man's rich, accented voice saying, "I know a thing. I will help."

As she lay in the lingering aftermath of it, she wondered if Mary Lou's recent memories of a certain young man had any connection to what happened to her brother—or to the frightful painting on his easel. Mercedes had seen strange things. People could bond in mysterious ways. At the very least, Mary Lou's subconscious mind might be stretching to recall something John once said that would comfort her.

Mercedes got dressed for whatever the day would bring, then sat down to soft, ambient music to work on a painting of a local historical scene. But thoughts of Doran Marlowe and the paintings in his large studio kept intruding.

Self-expression was not Mercedes' reason for painting. Her work contained no bold, unique statement about herself, no desire to establish a place for her vision in the world. Her goal was personal satisfaction and to share beautiful things, and she saw no purpose in making anything that would not please Jesus.

What drove Doran Marlowe to paint? Doctor Jansen Kirk owned a magnificent painting of an African waterfall by the artist, so apparently that view had touched Marlowe and moved him to interact with it.

In contrast, what Kirk saw on that easel yesterday surprised him. What inspired the explorer-turned-artist to paint a scene that was so out of character?

Once, she had been somewhere that was much like that painting. Only a ruin of it remained, and Quincy's father's team of archaeologists and anthropologists had researched the site and the people who used it. As a volunteer on that expedition, she hoped that what they discovered stayed in a museum she never planned to visit.

But being at the Marlowe house yesterday awakened a nagging dread inside her. Experiences work toward a purpose and were not random. Lessons learned today became the toolbox for tomorrow.

Mercedes joined Lois and Mary Lou for lunch. Lois was her tactful, practical self without ignoring that her friend was walking through a nightmare. Mary Lou was subdued and followed the motions and cues of those around her.

Wishing she was better at being a comfort to others, Mercedes said little rather than risk blurting out the wrong things. Mary Lou was her client from paperwork, a phone call, and their horrific meeting yesterday. But she wanted to go past that and be closer to her sister in Christ. How could she be the friend that a broken-hearted, grieving woman needed right now?

She marveled at spiritual gifts. People like Lois and her friends, and her pastor and his wife, seemed specially empowered to have the right words and actions when another believer needed them most.

Lois' cell phone chimed on the kitchen island, and she rushed to reach it before the caller must leave a message. She answered, then told Doran Marlowe's attorney that she would get Mary Lou to speak to him. Mary Lou took the phone with her into the living room.

"She knows nothing about her brother's will or his wishes about a funeral," whispered Lois. "We made tentative arrangements this morning. If he left nothing with his attorney, we may need to look for his safe or records at the house this afternoon."

"Is she going to be okay to go over there so soon?"

"It must be done, if not today, then tomorrow. We'll be with her."

"Lois, I haven't told you some things about the studio and about Doran's work. Mary Lou must not stay in the house alone yet."

Their friend came back into the kitchen, taking her seat again and handing Lois her phone. "Doran checked in with his attorney sometimes regarding the house, my contact information wherever I was working, and other financial matters. His will is simple, leaving all he had to me, and any arrangements for his funeral to me. He told his attorney all along that he expected to lose his life in some faraway place, never to return to Bluffton."

She put a hand to her trembling lips and closed her eyes against stinging tears. Her voice was hoarse when she said,

"That's just like him, to pass along anything he considered religious to me. He was a tough guy who didn't talk about his faith. Oh, I saw him walk through the typical salvation and baptism steps at our church when he was about twelve years old, and as an explorer, he studied the things people in other places worshipped. He treated those beliefs as curiosity. But he left no testimony of his faith that I know of. How am I to plan a funeral for him?"

Mercedes wished she had not heard this same lament so often, from friends who had no assurance to comfort them in the loss of a loved one. After years of encountering and confronting hopeless religions in the mission fields around the world, Mary Lou had returned home to find that her brother had an assortment of the same pagan idols she worked to free people from.

"He said they were only a collection of travel artifacts he wanted to write articles about and create sketches or paintings of for publications. But he knew better than to have them. I saw it in his eyes. Those things aren't harmless, and I made him lock the door from the house to the passage where they are. I prayed over it and hung a cross on the house side of the door."

She sniffed and waved a work-worn hand. "I'm sorry. This all sounds like a horror movie, doesn't it? Threatening vampires or werewolves with a cross!"

With a wan smile, she said, "I know there's no magic power in that cross-shaped wood and metal. I carried it around for years to hang in my tent or hut as a reminder that the power over other gods in Jesus, whose name is above all names, principalities, and territories. His death on a cross reversed the plans and purposes of the evil ones that roam the earth."

Lois took Mary Lou's hand across the small table. "You handled that well. As for Doran, there's reason for hope. Jesus has always been your strength and He won't fail you now. Most funerals are private here these days. Explain to the journalists who call you that because of the unexpected nature of Doran's passing, you need time to grieve. Tell them that later, you will share insights about his life."

Mary Lou sighed and thanked Lois for that advice. Then she looked at Mercedes. "I'm going to the house this afternoon to look for anything in Doran's room that will help me with what to say at his funeral. Will you please come with us? Perhaps you can get some work done while we go through his things."

Lois' phone chimed again, and she told the caller they would be right there. She rose so quickly from her seat that it almost tipped over. "That was an officer who was investigating at your house yesterday, Mary Lou. He didn't get an answer on your home phone, so he drove by to see if he could talk to you. A man was standing across the street, staring at your house. When he turned the car around to go question him, the man had disappeared. The officer asked us to meet him there as soon as we can."

A blinding flash from the badge on an officer's uniform made Mercedes wince and shade her eyes. She, Lois, and Mary Lou joined him and Dr. Kirk in the brilliant sunshine in front of the Marlowe house, where they all looked across the street to the park. The officer introduced himself, and Jensen Kirk put out his hand to shake theirs, nodding a greeting. He scowled in scrutiny of Mary Lou's face and asked if she was holding up okay.

The older woman sighed. "I don't know how 'okay' feels under the circumstances, Doctor, but Christian fellowship is holding me up and that's how I'll get through this. Let's move to the veranda for some shade."

When they were on the charming verandah, they followed the officer's lead and turned to survey the park again. Pointing to a spot near a street sign, he said a man was there earlier, watching the house. After the officer turned his car around and came back, the man was gone, but Dr. Kirk jogged up and reported seeing a man there as well.

"I don't want to alarm you, Miss Marlowe," the officer said. "He was probably just a curious local who heard about your brother, or a tourist who found the house interesting. But because of what happened yesterday, I wanted to find out. I thought you might be at home."

"Can you describe the man? Perhaps I know him."

The officer looked at Dr. Kirk, who said, "We compared notes and have the same description. The man was dark complexioned, I would guess South American. He wore a light-colored broad-brimmed hat, jeans and a loose fitting white short-sleeve shirt that buttoned up the front."

"His height was about medium, and I noticed he wore a silver watch and dark athletic shoes," added the officer.

Mary Lou gasped and reached for Lois' arm. All eyes turned to her, but then followed her searching gaze across the street to the park. She asked, "Where did you see him?"

The officer and Dr. Kirk pointed to the same area, but all they saw were children laughing and playing games. No one matching the suspicious man's description was around.

Mary Lou's eyes lit up with wonder. "An old friend in South America who keeps coming to my mind could fit the same description."

Mercedes caught her breath. "You mean the one who tells you he knows something and can help you?"

"Yes! But—that makes no sense, does it? What on earth would he be doing here?"

The officer scowled and glanced at Dr. Kirk, who pushed his sunglasses up onto his head and scrutinized Mercedes. Then the officer turned to Mary Lou and chose his words carefully. "Miss Marlowe, are you saying someone in South America that you've been thinking about recently is talking to you in your thoughts, and he could be the man in the park looking at your house today?"

His tone was professional. But the words hung in the humid air around them, haunting them with the absurdity they suggested.

Mary Lou sighed, hesitating. Then she closed her eyes, put her hands to her face, and wearily rubbed her temples.

Mercedes hooked her arm through Mary Lou's and suggested that she should get out of the heat and rest. "If we need to tidy any loose ends with you, officer, you may come in and we'll try to help."

Dr. Kirk rushed to open the front screen door for them, while the officer hesitated, uncertain whether he wanted to pursue the turn his questions had taken. "Oh, that's unnecessary," he said. "Dr. Kirk, you have my card if anything helpful comes up."

Doran Marlowe furnished the front living room of his house with modern comfort in mind. Taken aback, Dr. Kirk stopped just inside the door and looked around. Mercedes snatched up a soft ocean-blue throw pillow and waited for her friend to settle into a gray leather recliner.

She smiled at Dr. Kirk's surprise and tucked the pillow behind Mary Lou's head. "Doran bought durable things when he came back. He planned for Mary Lou's retirement here with him, so she would have a ministry with their boarding guests and vacationers. But he only furnished the main living areas and two small suites he was renting, so she could select the rest. His plan was to live in his studio while Mary Lou remodeled and redecorated, and that's why she hired me."

More understanding was dawning in Dr. Kirk's eyes with each passing minute. "That's what you do—help with remodeling?"

Mercedes chuckled and moved away from Mary Lou's recliner. Lois bent to switch on an air cleaner in a corner near built-in bookcases laden with titles about world travel.

"You could think of it that way. But I'm not an interior decorator, nor am I a contractor. I handle evaluations and reports, doing archival research and historic building assessments. My clients are usually either preparing to meet regulations to run a business from their historic properties, such as a bed-and-breakfast and boarding, or they are looking to get the property on the historic registries and keep their upgrades within the standards of preservation. They consider themselves stewards of history."

She nodded toward the air cleaner, which whispered in the corner. "Mary Lou uses the air filter because she's bothered by the mustiness in the house that's common to aging structures. When my work is done and she hires a remodeling expert, she won't have that problem any longer. She can just rely on the air filter for seasonal pollen issues."

But the look in his keen eyes as she met them told her he was unsatisfied. It was inadequate for the interest Officer Cordero had shown yesterday when she gave him her name, and Kirk was not buying her boring career description.

Lois asked him to watch Mary Lou while she got everyone some tea, and he agreed to sit with her while she napped.

Mercedes and Lois went down the foyer toward the kitchen, but Mercedes stopped abruptly and took a quick step back.

"What is it? You act like you hit a wall," Lois asked. Then Lois followed Mercedes' wide eyes and saw a closed door behind a kitchen cart where Mary Lou stored a toaster oven and other counter appliances. A worn old cross on a leather strap hung on a hook in the top middle panel of the door, incongruous among the everyday tools for preparing food.

Lois whispered so Mary Lou would not overhear them. "Is this the door Mary Lou talked about? I'm not sure I'd have noticed it, Mercedes. How did you know?"

Mercedes shook her head, staring at the door and trying to clear away the memory of a spooky warning she had years ago on a dig site in Peru. She cleared her throat and swallowed hard. "I'm not sure. As you said, it felt like I bumped into a wall. Lois, did you hear anything?"

"A scraping sound, I think. I assumed it was from the street. What did you hear?"

"I heard a—a snarl."

Lois uttered a soft cry of dismay. "Oh, no. Mary Lou was right about the souvenirs Doran collected, wasn't she? Is this what you meant at lunch today, about something you haven't told me and that she can't come back here alone yet?"

Mercedes nodded. Another memory was flooding her mind. It was of a sketch on the bottom of a page in her Great-Great Grand Aunt Mercedes' journal. She had meant to get back to it, but several weeks had flown by and it lay untouched on a table in her cottage.

I know a thing. I can help. The words from her dream this morning ran like news ticker tape through her mind. Or was it because they were fresh in her memory from Mary Lou's speculation about her old friend to the police officer and Dr. Kirk?

She and Lois jumped when her phone chimed to alert her to a text message. She took another step back, eyes riveted on the door and the cross. Lois shooed her out with a motion of her hands, telling her to answer her phone and assuring her she could manage the refreshments tray alone.

When Mercedes spun on her heel back to the living room to go outside, she bumped into Dr. Kirk. His running shoes had muffled his steps as he came close behind her.

Flustered, she untangled herself from his steadying arms and muttered an automatic apology, excusing herself as she rushed past him. She glanced at the recliner on her way to the front door to see Mary Lou's eyes were closed.

Dr. Kirk silently followed her out the front door and quietly pulled it closed, so as not to wake Mary Lou. Surprised, Mercedes whirled around. "Is Mary Lou all right?"

He stared hard at her, eyes narrowed, and she wanted to shrink back. Still shaken and flushed, she stood motionless, her heart pounding and her mind praying. *Lord, show me what to say.*

"Who are you?" he asked with a steely voice.

Mercedes blinked. "I—I told you that. Yesterday."

He almost sneered and made a soft snorting noise. "Oh yeah, you gave us your name and your relationship to the Marlowe's. I learned more about you last night on the internet, in this summer's online news posts. Today, you explained in broad terms what your profession is. Help me out here, Miss Mercedes Annalee Ellison. I'm trying not to let my mind fill in between the lines, but I can't deny what I just saw happen. Nobody can fake that, and you had no reason to. Who are you, and what was that?"

She started and gasped when her phone rang. Looking down at the screen, she said, "Excuse me, I have to take this." She put her phone to her ear and walked toward the other side of the veranda. "Hi, Quincy."

Behind her, the screen door creaked open, and the front door closed. She glanced back in relief to see the empty veranda.

Quincy's warm greeting was like a hug, and Mercedes closed her eyes. She felt shaky as she sank into the welcoming cushions of a creaking white wicker rocking chair. The arms embraced her, and the afternoon sunshine slatted through the porch railing onto her tanned legs and sandals, spotlighting the iridescent glimmer in her teal pedicure polish.

Everything out here was safe, humdrum, normal. This was what a lazy summer day should be. This is what she longed for her life to be like.

"I sent a text in case it is a bad time to catch you," Quincy was saying. "I'll be late today. There's a dreadful accident on I-95, and I'm backed up in traffic for miles. I can't be there for dinner unless we eat late. Maybe we can have dessert around the pool tonight?"

"Oh. Sure. That's disappointing for us and sad for whoever is involved. Please take your time and relax. I just want you to—be here."

Mercedes traced a finger over the outlines of a palm frond pattern on the chair cushion, feeling disconnected from this conversation and ready to tell her friends that she was going back to her cottage to rest.

"Mercedes? Where are you, and what happened?"

She sighed, and her voice was lethargic. "I'm at the Marlowe house, with Mary Lou and Lois. A police officer called us as we finished lunch, reporting that a man was watching the house. We ended up inside when Mary Lou felt faint, and she's napping now. I'm not sure yet what happened to me in the house, but I'm getting away once I end this call. I'll be ready to talk about it when you get home."

He groaned, and she heard a sound like a slap of his hand on his leather car console. "Please tell me you took Aaron or the pastor inside with you, as I asked."

"Aaron is supposed to arrive any time. Dr. Kirk is here with us, though. He's the physician who came to help when we heard the screams from the house yesterday. He was jogging by again as the officer was driving past, and they both noticed a man watching the house. But Quincy, none of them would have prevented or understood what happened to me a few minutes ago."

With a sigh, she rubbed her forehead. "I'm fine, but I suddenly feel drained, like Mary Lou did earlier. I'll say goodbye to Lois and get back to my cottage."

"This really makes me uneasy, Mercedes. It's strange that both you and Mary Lou had these physical reactions at the house within a short time. Call me when you get home, so I'll know you are okay. Get some rest and I'll keep you posted about what time I'll be there."

Chapter 4

Mercedes wondered at the unusual lethargy she felt. After texting Quincy that she was back at her cottage and would rest, she curled up on the sofa to search her Great-Great Grand Aunt's journal. As always, the elusive, beguiling scent of roses wafted from the aging pages of the book. She dreaded what the words written in faded periwinkle ink might reveal, but she must know if a trail of strange sand was trickling through time, through her family, from this journal entry. Was this relevant to what happened to her years ago, and to what happened today at the Marlow house?

The page she needed to see was not far ahead of where a teal satin ribbon was saving her place. Mercedes found the small sketch under a brief entry, and her heart raced. There was no date noted before her Great-Great Grand Aunt's words.

My beloved grandmother spent her lifetime preparing me to recognize evil and lean on Jesus for protection and guidance. If she ever encountered what I did today, Jesus was all she had, for her silver and garlic was no help.

The natives we share the Gospel with say this cave door I am sketching is a portal to another world where the tribe's gods live, and they set up small idols of them in niches around the opening. The statues have no physical life in them, but the entities they represent have a powerful spiritual presence. We can sense it when we are nearby.

Today, I passed by the door with some of my native friends. By the time my husband rushed to help me rise from the ground where we all fell, my friends and I could only say something blocked us from going any further. A presence which I cannot describe gave me the impression of a powerful warning. I am hated by an entity I cannot fathom, and if this entity has the power it claims to have, the lives of my loved ones will be in jeopardy. For I cannot do as it demands. I will not stop living the Great Commission and following my family's path.

At my cry to Jesus for help, the darkness vaporized into the shadows of the cave. My husband assures me nothing can harm him until the Lord allows it, but I tremble when I recall the warning.

I pray that the Lord's will is done on earth as it is in heaven. Amen.

It was the texting alert on her cell phone that awakened Mercedes from a long nap. Her drowsy eyes peeked open to see late rays of sunlight and deepening shadows spilling through the French doors, enveloping her and the comfortable sofa where she lay.

Unwilling to leave the peace of restfulness, she lay still. If she rose, she would move forward, taking the next step.

That was a step too far. She preferred to remain here, in safety.

But a knock on her door shattered the lazy peace she relished, and she stirred. When it came briskly, she sighed and sat up. Quincy's voice sounded alarmed as she heard him on the other side of the door.

"Mercedes! Come on, you're scaring me! Lois said you're in here."

As she reached the door, her phone was ringing back on the sofa table, and when she opened it to answer, Quincy stood there with his phone near his ear. He ended the call with a long sigh of relief, appraising her disheveled state. "Mercedes, what's going on?"

She stood in the doorway and opened her mouth to offer some explanation or reassurance. But her mind was blank. Not knowing where to begin, or how to explain, all she could do was to gulp back tears.

He wrapped his arms around her. It was the safest place she could expect right now, so without knowing why, she cried.

The salad Lois brought out to the poolside table for Quincy and Mercedes was a hearty one. Both refrigerators were bursting with food from her prayer circle group. She also brought out a small cooler containing gluten-free brownies with dairy-free ice cream, and it was a luxurious meal.

But it was a change in plans for Quincy, who had arrived thinking his excuse for hanging out by the pool with his fiancée was dessert and relaxing with a swim. After Mercedes finally stopped crying, he learned that she had not eaten. He sat her down at a table and knocked on Lois' back door.

He looked out the window over the kitchen sink to check on Mercedes while he and Lois raided the refrigerator. She pulled out the makings of two salads topped with citrus marinated chicken as she told him a brief version of what happened at the Marlowe house that afternoon. Since Mary Lou was in the guest bedroom suite having a shower, Lois kept her voice down for Quincy's ears only. Then she sent him back out to sit with Mercedes while she put the salads and dessert together.

Between bites, Quincy brought Mercedes up to date on progress at the dig site, where the team was successful at finding artifacts to support pirate activity. Mercedes asked questions that proved she was listening and connecting how the items fit into the big picture his team was hoping for. But otherwise, she was silent and seemed fatigued.

After dinner, they sat in the lounge chairs by the pool, where the water glowed turquoise with underwater lighting and always made him think of the water around the Florida Keys. Overhead, the first stars were beginning to sparkle, which was the cue the insects waited for to begin their nightly concert. Lanterns around the pool and garden made palms and tropical foliage glow and cast eerie shadows.

Reaching over to take Mercedes' hand, Quincy prayed silently for guidance about helping her talk through her ordeal. While sitting in traffic on the way back, he had called her brother to give him the nutshell version of what little he knew. He asked him what he recalled about the dig site they worked near Cusco, Peru, when Mercedes encountered something that not only scared her, but scarred her.

At seventeen years old, that was a turning point for Mercedes. He had assumed they would get married someday and she would accompany him on dig sites around the world, as his mother had done with his father. He had imagined them raising and homeschooling their children on those travels. Then something happened to her that changed everything.

After that day, Mercedes started searching for a career path that protected her from the strange things that occurred on pagan dig sites. Quincy felt dismayed at this threat to their plan of traveling the world together during his career as an archaeologist. Eventually, she asked him to join her permanently in America. Furious and disappointed, he had chosen archaeology and turned away.

On the phone, her brother Zeke remembered sketchy details about the accomplishments of the mission in Peru. But what he always thought of when he recalled the trip was the strange sense of evil that he had around the carving at the cave door and what happened to his sister. He also reminded Quincy that by the end of that expedition, their parents were never enthusiastic about a match between Quincy and Mercedes.

Despite the obstacles over the past few years, they were now a couple and planned to marry. But now he understood they didn't leave the past behind, and, as absurd as it seemed, it followed them all the way to Bluffton, South Carolina.

Idly, he ran his thumb gently up and down over the softness on the back of her hand, silently admiring the engagement ring he had given her. "Do you feel like talking or going for a swim?"

"Talking is inevitable," she said after a sigh. "I'll try, and then maybe we'll take a break to relax and swim. But I hardly know where to begin. I believe you'll see more than I do if you go to the Marlowe house with me tomorrow."

"Lois told me what she saw today, and about the reason you were all called there. I don't understand why you're in so deep with this, and it would help if you told me how you knew about the man watching Mary Lou's house, and why you balked and wouldn't go into the kitchen."

Mercedes looked off into a rustling palm, where a green lizard scurried around the trunk to the shadows. "Lois, her pastor, and I were sitting with Mary Lou in the living room here last night, keeping her talking. You know, a distraction, doing something normal and calming, so she can get past the shock and be able to sleep."

Quincy nodded understanding while she continued. "The pastor asked about her missionary days, and eventually she brought up an account of a young man in South America who became a genuine believer. He was hungry to learn the Bible. The young man was the son of a witch doctor, or shaman, or whatever they called the divination chief there. He wanted to be baptized and renamed John. She said that John had been on her mind lately."

Mercedes stopped and looked into Quincy's eyes. "I don't know why, but—I believe that somehow, this man is important. I asked Mary Lou what he's doing when he comes to mind, and it's always the same thing. She said he tells her he knows something and can help. He calls her 'Lulu,' the name all the young people in the tribe called her."

Looking down now at her hand in Quincy's, she squeezed. "I slept in this morning, and just before a boom of thunder made the cottage tremble and awakened me, I dreamed of a man saying, 'I know a thing. I will help.'"

She grinned lopsidedly and looked up. "Oh, I know. Her story moved me and was fresh in my mind, that accounts for the dream. But what if there's a connection? It's no secret that sometimes people who are close can know what the other is thinking. It happens with us, right? I am thinking about you calling and my phone rings. And when the officer described the man watching the house, I just knew it wasn't a criminal involved in Doran's death. I believe it was John. So did Mary Lou."

Quincy studied her and nodded. "You believe John knows what happened to Doran and wants to rescue Mary Lou."

Mercedes sighed, looking into his eyes. "Yes. And he's traveled a long way in a short time. I know how this sounds, Quincy, but she's spent a lifetime in places where strange things are normal."

Quincy looked up at the moon, then laced his fingers through hers. "You wonder if John knew something and was on his way before Doran passed away in his studio."

"I do, and I hope he will come back to the house and shed light on this mystery. Wouldn't it be just like Jesus to send help to Mary Lou in the most unexpected way? She isn't even certain about her brother's salvation, because like many men in his generation, he was quiet about it. Before the police called about the stranger watching the house, Mary Lou had asked Lois and me to go there with her. She planned to look through Doran's things for any hint of his faith or last wishes for his funeral."

"So, you *were* going to head over there without Aaron or the pastor?"

Mercedes returned his teasing smile. "I knew Aaron was planning to arrive early in the afternoon. But then the officer called Lois and asked us to come right then. I didn't know Dr. Kirk was there—that was providential, since Mary Lou suddenly felt so weak. But...I'm just not sure about him, Quincy."

He leaned her way to bump her shoulder with his. "Every time his name comes up, you become evasive. I suppose he's nonchalant, brilliant, and extremely fit. Should I be jealous?"

"Ouch—you caught me. You know my taste for brilliance, but I already have that in you. Plus, you have a charming, warm personality and you take care of yourself, but you're not obsessive about it. You have incredible eyes, frank, missing nothing, and yet vulnerable. When you look at me, they turn sweet."

He searched her face for signs of teasing, and then quipped, "Okay, I think I get it now. His obsession with fitness cancels out his brilliance. He looks like he runs marathons and drinks protein and kale shakes. He has a stereotypical aloof physician's demeanor. But the only difference in our eyes is that he's not vulnerable or sweet when he looks at you."

Mercedes blinked. Then she looked away, her mind racing.

"Hey," Quincy said solemnly. "What's this all about?"

With her free hand, Mercedes pulled her hair behind her ear and ran it down the length of her hair, staring at the pool. After a few moments, she said, "No, that's not the only difference. Your eyes are a wonderful, intense blue. His eyes are gray, like they didn't commit to a color, and piercing, like he's searching for secrets. And he's investigating mine every time he looks at me."

"What? How do you know?"

"I just do. And because he asked me outright today, before I answered your call. He watched me from the living room and saw what happened."

Mercedes leaned her head back on the lounge chair pillow and closed her eyes. "Remember when I told you that when

Officer Cordero asked for my identification, he recognized my name? That surprised Dr. Kirk and stirred his curiosity. He saw Cordero watching me at the house, when I suddenly knew something was wrong with the connecting passage to the studio. Remember how Cordero came to catch up with me and asked why I had stopped? Kirk was watching us."

Quincy sat up straighter, and she opened her eyes to find his. Then she told him about how Dr. Kirk had followed and confronted her about what happened in the house.

"What did he see, Mercedes? What spooked him?"

"Well...I was walking with Lois and felt as if I bumped into a wall. I heard an unearthly snarl. The barrier wasn't physical, yet it stopped me, and not Lois. She said she heard a rumble. There was a cross on a door ahead of me, which was blocked by a kitchen cart with appliances on it. I've heard or imagined the sound before, encountered the barrier before, and felt the same dread before. The cross was one Mary Lou told us about at lunch. She put it there and locked the door. It leads to the passageway where her brother stores a collection of pagan souvenirs."

With another gentle squeeze of her hand in his, Quincy scowled and studied her face. "Would Mary Lou know if Doran had been in Peru?"

Mary Lou gazed out of the kitchen window over the sink at Lois's house. From behind her, Lois stopped her chit-chat about their dinner and recipes to look at the couple enjoying a swim in her courtyard pool.

With a slight turn of her head to acknowledge Lois, Mary Lou said softly, "Seeing them together makes me long for something I don't even understand. Romance passed me by, but I trust it is the Lord's will for me. Is that her young man?"

"Hmmm. Yes. I hope you'll get to know Quincy, he's such an interesting person. He's been to many places, raised on archaeological sites, and as solid a Christian man as you can pray for at so young an age. And to top it all off, he's got a British accent. Not a strong one, his mother is American, but most of his dealings were around the English."

"How did they meet?"

"Oh, not sure about that. They met as children, both from old English family lines who have connected for generations. But her side of the Ellison family left for America in the early nineteen-hundreds. I'm old friends with Mercedes' mother. That's why she's here in my cottage this summer. The kids, they don't realize I know about their heritage. Mystery and horror fiction authors found inspiration in the stories of strange encounters that happened within the Ellison and Holmwood family generations. Mercedes and Quincy prefer few people know that, but she won't mind if you do. You're likely to have stories yourself and aren't the type to go to the news with it."

Mary Lou's expression was quizzical. "Quincy and Holmwood."

With a grin, Lois finished drying two dessert plates and handed them to her. She hung the dish towel on a rack and said, "Yes, he has an American namesake from a classic horror novel, and his own last name from the same book."

Mary Lou glanced out the window again, then shook her head in wonder. "What a fascinating world it is. So, Mercedes and Quincy have been a couple all these years?"

"Oh, they broke the relationship off for a while, and she tried another, but to say things didn't work out is an understatement. That ended the week she came to stay here for the summer, after opening some documents in a hidden panel within an old cedar chest that she picked up at an estate auction. Turned out that the chest had belonged to her ancestor, her namesake, and they lost it when being shipped to America. Quincy was investigating her boyfriend's new employer for antiquities theft and trying to remain incognito. What she learned prepared her to accept what happened. Let's go into the living room and I'll tell you all about it."

Chapter 5

The early birds were singing and fluttering in the bird bath outside of Quincy's cottage as he leaned back into his desk chair with a cup of strong English tea. He watched the birds, then turned to look over records on a computer monitor screen, waiting for his parents' housekeeper to bring his dad to the phone. It was a busy time for his parents, he knew, as they got his grandparents settled in a detached guest house at their home in Charleston.

He sipped the warm tea and heard two voices in the background, unaware there was a landline phone off the cradle with a caller waiting. At first, their conversation was indistinct, but he recognized his grandparents' voices.

"Well, you are right, the girl is a dear, ordinarily a beautiful match," said his grandfather. "Tiffany loves Mercedes and the Ellisons, so she's excited about the wedding. But honestly, thinking about what might happen keeps me up at night sometimes. It's one thing to be linked with the distinguished English side of the Ellison family in the past, but mixing our blood is another matter altogether. The girl is delightful and lovely, but I'll take ordinary over those things any day. What manner of freaks might our great-grandchildren be? I tell you, the Holmwood legacy is on the line."

"Shhh," said his grandmother. "Keep your voice down. Perhaps the children won't be special at all. Besides, no legacy exists for the Holmwoods outside of England, dear. What does a wedding in this part of the world look like? What does the groom's grandmother wear to a porch or a swamp wedding?"

"You mean a marsh, my dear. Not a swamp, if there's a difference. I saw some local news about places named for the Swamp Fox, who must have been a daring champion of the colonies."

By the time he heard his father's voice greeting his grandparents and picking up the phone, Quincy's jaw clenched with tension. "Good morning, dad. Everybody doing well as you settle in today?"

"Oh, it's too early to say, but the furniture is on schedule to be delivered to the villa for Mum and Dad in an hour. On Lowcountry time, that means at least two hours or more, if it does in fact arrive at all. I'll keep you posted, or you can check in later."

Quincy chuckled and set down his empty cup. "I have some stories about adventures in Lowcountry time, too, but it's no worse than South American time."

His dad laughed outright. "True! What am I complaining about?"

"Listen, Dad, speaking of South America, do you remember much about the last site we worked in Peru?"

There was a noticeable change in his father's manner. "Well. Well, that was a while back."

Quincy grimaced and rolled his chair closer to the computer screen. "It seems like it. But it isn't when you see the dates in the reports, which I'm looking over right now. I recall logging in more information in our records than this version has. Photos are missing, as well. Just wanted to check to be sure you knew about it."

His father cleared his throat, then asked him to wait a few moments. Quincy heard him ask his grandparents to give him privacy, and their fading voices left the room.

In a business tone of voice, his father said, "I worked with Dawson to keep the report clean but accurate. Much happens on a dig site that has no place in the sponsor's records. They only want the results and the research."

Quincy scowled and pursed his lips. Then he found the right words to respond. "Even if it might link to an artifact discovered years down the road?"

He smiled ruefully to himself as his dad gasped and stammered. "Well, I don't see—exactly what are you saying?"

"I'm saying I want access to the photos and records you and Dawson Ellison kept off the sponsor report. Zeke Ellison can bring them to me when he comes down to help, or you and Dawson can show up. If they're in a digital format, just send them to me online. Something came up, and I took a few days off from the dig in St. Augustine to investigate a stash of artifacts collected by an explorer and guide named Doran Marlowe. Ever hear of him?"

Mercedes slept deeply after her evening talking to and swimming with Quincy. He was planning on working until noon, then they would return to the Marlowe house with Mary Lou and Lois. She could complete the needed reports for the remodeling paperwork without going into the kitchen or passage, but she could not simply walk away from the job and leave Mary Lou to live there. In her prayers, she was asking for help to determine what to do about the presence she felt in the house.

After puttering through the cottage to shower and make breakfast, she hoped to finish a painting on her easel. There were texts from friends, but she replied to them saying she was busy with work and would catch up in a few days. Sometimes there was no comfortable way to talk about things that were happening in her life.

Before she dipped her brush into paint, her brother phoned. Smiling, she answered, "Good morning, Zeke. It's your day off, so I hope you're relaxing."

He laughed, an easy, contagious sound that warmed her heart. "You know what the old saying is. No rest for the weary, especially when I hang out with you and your sidekick."

"What?"

A brisk knock peppered the cottage door, and Zeke said, "Open up. It's just me."

She rushed to turn the knob and stood with her phone still held to her ear, staring in disbelief at her brother. He grinned and ended the call, sliding his phone into the pocket of a pair of khaki cargo shorts. She laid her phone on the countertop, opening her arms to hug him.

"Why didn't you tell me you were coming?" she asked, on tiptoe with her chin on his shoulder. "Come in out of the heat. Have you had breakfast?"

He followed her inside. "Of course! Grandma doesn't let me leave the house without being fed, no matter the hour. And before you ask, traffic was nuts. I don't know how many people travel 'holiday road' in a season, but hordes of vacationers zipped down this morning."

"August is busy because families are getting a last vacation to the beach before school starts again," Mercedes replied.

Zeke noticed her travel easel set up and went over to look at her work while he answered her first question. "Quincy's bein' bossy about you gettin' enough rest after what happened to Doran Marlowe, and he told me not to call and wake you up. So, I just drove down and let you sleep."

As she considered this news, he studied her painting. "I like it. Looks much better than the reference photo. Your vision for the scene is fresh."

Then he turned a searching look into her eyes. "I want to see Doran's studio, Mercedes. The painting he was working on, the ones he covered up, and whether he used reference photos, painted from memory, or—through channeling."

Staring back at her brother, Mercedes gulped and slowly sank to the nearby sofa. "Okay. Well—he may have included objects he collected and sent home from his travels. I think—if Dr. Kirk is around, I think he would like to see them, too, and Mary Lou trusts him to go out to the studio with you."

Crossing his arms, Zeke studied her and sighed. "I'm not sure we can sort this out without you."

Mercedes squeezed her eyes shut and covered her face in her hands. After a few moments, she met her brother's gaze. She almost whispered as she said, "Zeke, what happened to me has happened before. I just learned that my namesake's journal recorded something eerily similar when she spent time with her husband on the mission field in the early 1900s, before he died in World War I. The entry was so brief that I might easily have overlooked it, except that she did a sketch of a cave opening at the bottom of the page."

Startled, Zeke came to settle beside her on the sofa. "There's something you never told me and Quincy?"

When she looked down at the coastal pattern on the area rug and nodded, he wiped his hands over his face and groaned. Finally, he said, "I reminded Quincy yesterday that something changed between our families on that dig, and my gut told me it was about that incident. When I told Dad last night that I was coming here today to check on you and help Quincy evaluate a stash of Doran Marlowe's artifacts, he looked relieved. Then, as I was leaving this morning, he got a call from Jonathan. I said goodbye, and the look on his face unsettled me. I hesitated, thinking he had bad news, but he just told Jonathan to hold on a minute. He gave me a strange look and told me to be alert and careful down here, text him when I arrived, and to stay in touch."

Turning to her, Zeke asked, "What's stoppin' you from telling me and Quincy what Dad and Jonathan know?"

Mercedes stood quickly and crossed her arms, pacing the room and looking out the French doors to the pool. "I wanted to believe I imagined it all, that it wasn't real. And until Doran Marlowe's death, it didn't come to mind any more. I thought it was an awful experience with relevance only to that time and place, not something that would follow me. Aren't pagan spirits territorial?"

Slowly, he rose from his seat on the sofa and stared at her. "Mercedes, there were witnesses who saw what happened and ended up on the ground like you did. Was your experience different from theirs? I didn't hear reports of a threat."

Both started at Quincy's confident knock on her door. Mercedes' hand instinctively went to her hair to tidy it while she cleared her throat, and Zeke's long stride took him to the door to invite his friend inside. He half-smiled at the special look his best friend always had for his sister, and waited while they greeted one another with a hug.

"Can I get you anything?" Mercedes asked.

Quincy raked back his damp hair. "It was a short but sweltering walk here. Do you have any of those flavored sparkling waters in the fridge?"

"Always. You too, Zeke?" Mercedes moved past her brother to the kitchen.

"Uh, yeah, the lemon or lime kind if you've got one," he replied at her back. Then he settled comfortably in a chair with seagulls flying over the printed fabric while Quincy took a seat on the sofa and made small talk about Zeke's drive down from Charleston.

Mercedes set out mosaic tile coasters and pretty glasses with lemon slices floating in bubbly fizzing water. Then she settled next to Quincy. The conversation about the weather and traffic trailed off, and Zeke turned a long, searching look to his sister.

Quincy pursed his lips. "Everything okay? Did I interrupt something?"

Mercedes sighed, then rose and left the room. With a lifted brow, Quincy shot a questioning look at her brother and put his half-empty glass on the coaster. Zeke nodded but said nothing as she returned, clutching a small book close to her heart. She went to his chair and handed it to him.

Quincy squirmed to the edge of the sofa. Mercedes said, "As an Ellison, Zeke should be the first to read this, but then he can share it with you. The entry is at the bookmarker."

She went to sit by Quincy again, picking up her water with both hands and sipping it nervously. Zeke read the journal entry, then handed the book across the table to Quincy.

Opening the marked page, Quincy's head jerked up. "That's a drawing of the portal!"

"Yes. Or a similar one. What happened to Mercedes also happened years ago to her namesake, our Great-Great Grand Aunt Mercedes. This isn't the first time—in fact, we don't know how many times or places it has happened to my family or anyone else. Maybe even to Doran Marlowe."

Incredulous, Quincy's eyes lingered on the ominous words in faded ink. He looked up at Zeke, then to Mercedes. "Are you telling us you also heard this—this—"

His hand went up in a helpless gesture while he searched for the right word. "You heard a warning? Does my family know this?"

Mercedes nodded slowly, then Zeke told him about the call between their fathers before he left Charleston that morning. "My dad emphasized being alert and careful and asked me to text him when I arrived here, which I did. You know this is not a habit of his, keeping tabs on me."

Putting the book down on the table, Quincy went to look out at the pool, rubbing the nape of his neck with his hands. For a few minutes, the room was quiet. Mercedes met Zeke's eyes, and he mouthed, *"It's okay."*

Quincy spoke to the view outside. "What am I supposed to do with this?"

With a sigh of exasperation, Zeke retorted, "For a start, you could come sit down and have a conversation, as I was doing before you walked in. I was about to find out the specifics on what Mercedes heard."

Whirling around, Quincy's heated tone made Mercedes wince. "The years of confusion I endured about what changed in my family after that expedition were totally unnecessary! Telling me the truth would've explained why Mercedes suddenly became an awkward subject and why my dad and grandparents became distant when I started our relationship up again."

His tone was defiant when he went to stand in front of her, hands on his hips. "Why did you keep this secret from me?"

Misery was in Mercedes' eyes when she held his. "Your dad, mine, and the site supervisor interviewed each person separately. I told them all I could remember, not knowing what any of the others reported. Until they asked me to repeat what I heard, I didn't realize I was the only one who mentioned a message. Your dad's expression—he looked at me like I'm a freak, then turned away to hide his face. But I noticed, and so did my dad. They went off into a huddle, whispering, and I saw by my dad's motions that he was protesting."

She gulped and glanced at Zeke and back to Quincy. "They finally came to my seat and told me my story was like the others and they believed me, but no one else heard any words or had the impression of a message. They only heard a rumbling sound. Quincy, your dad said the official report would not mention my personal encounter. He asked me not to tell you about the threat, since it could well have been my imagination."

After a pause for a deep breath, she said, "My dad took my arm as we left the tent. I saw fury in his eyes and his voice was gruff when he said, 'Never waste your life and love on anyone who doesn't think you're extraordinary, Mercedes.' You never treated me like I was ordinary, Quincy, but I'm not the normal woman your dad wanted for you. So, I honored his request. If I really heard a threat about my loved ones, I didn't want to put you in danger. And frankly, at that point, I never wanted to risk a creepy encounter on another pagan dig site. You planned to spend your life in them."

Quincy's angry flush and flashing eyes spoke for him. He turned to Zeke. "I'm going home to get some work done. Call me when Lois and Mary Lou are ready to go to the Marlowe house."

Without a backward glance, he left the cottage. It surprised Mercedes that the door did not slam.

Zeke stared after him and rolled his eyes. "He's not really upset at you, Mercedes, it's about his dad. Let him pray about this on his own and blow off some steam. If he doesn't adjust his attitude soon, I'll remind him of some things he's kept from you, too."

Mercedes sighed and wearily rubbed her forehead, wondering what Quincy might hide from her or had forgotten to tell her. Her brother reached for the old journal again and leafed through a few pages at the beginning.

Putting his finger on a spot, he said, "I think it's a good time for you to remember something written in here when you first started reading this. Great-Great Grand Aunt Mercedes wrote about her last evening with her grandmother, Claire, before Roland murdered her. Claire Ellison had often taught Mercedes simple lessons about spiritual warfare from the Bible, and Mercedes hoped the Lord would send her a like-minded spouse so they could be like the purifying bulbs of garlic pairs that Claire was binding with three strands of cord that night, to represent the Trinity. She hoped to marry someone to travel life's roads with, sent out two by two, like Jesus sent His disciples."

Zeke now had all Mercedes' attention. She sat still, watching his face, and he tapped a spot on the journal page. "But you know what really grabbed me when you showed me this story a couple of months ago? It was the ending. Great-Great Grand Aunt Mercedes hints at the many legends about Claire Ellison, who lived in a vastly different time and in a rural English countryside."

He looked into her eyes. "Listen to this. If it doesn't make your heart surge with courage, sister, I don't know whatever could." He looked down and started reading, *"My grandmother's roads are now in the past, and I am not likely to walk them. But she warned me about an enemy that is not limited to space or time until Jesus returns. She has prepared me for my own encounters because I am entrusted with a legacy of power, strength, and wisdom."*

He paused for a deep breath, then blew it out and cleared his throat to read the last line. But Mercedes had memorized it, and she said it along with him. *"I am Mercedes Ellison, and I cannot escape my destiny."*

Rubbing his temples did not ease the tension there, and Quincy expected a headache to invade his day. He stuffed back his anger and throbbing hurt about being deceived. Mostly, he was upset with his father, and what Mercedes revealed about the agreement was in his character. Jonathan Holmwood could not deny things he had experienced with the Ellisons, but Quincy saw the resistance in his demeanor. It was just like him insisting on not recording anything supernatural in the records of the dig.

He needed to sort through his feelings about what he had learned before he talked to his dad about his role in asking Mercedes not to tell him the truth. And as for Mercedes, she had been only seventeen at the time of the dig. She deserved some grace for obeying their father's requests, but it hurt him she agreed with his dad to deceive him. Was this the only time such a thing had happened? How many other things was she hiding from him, and did they come to mind when she accepted his engagement ring? If Doran Marlowe had not died, they might have married with this between them.

There were still a few things he needed to do before joining Zeke and Mercedes in an investigation at the Marlowe house. With a grunt, he settled his office chair up to his desk and picked up his phone, then texted a friend. *Something has come up. Any chance you can trade weeks with me to lead the Bible Study?*

He glanced at a nearby planner he used to stay organized, studying the calendar to brainstorm reschedules. A notification sounded on his phone, and he selected the response from his friend. *Are you a mind reader? My mother-in-law will visit next weekend and my sweetheart made a honey-do list longer than my arm. No way I could do all that and the research the same week, so let's trade. Hey, everything okay?*

Quincy rubbed his temple with his free hand, then typed an answer. *I want to say yeah. But I'm not sure. Lots of strange sand flowing through the hourglass here. Pray for me to be alert and wise. I'll be in touch soon.*

He was sending the text when his phone trembled in his hand with another notification. It was his dad.

Quincy braced himself, checked the message, and read it. *I talked to Dawson this morning, but Zeke was on his way out. Dawson and I agreed I need to tell you something before I release any of the information that you're asking me for. If you get a break from work, call me.*

He stared at the words and a new text from his dad came through. *Listen, avoid any risky situations right now. Stay on high alert, just as if you're on a dig site.*

"Adventure Awaits" By Pamela Poole

Chapter 6

When Zeke, Mercedes, and Mary Lou arrived at the Marlowe house in Lois' car, Quincy and Lois' friend Aaron were standing in the driveway, eyeing the passage to the garage studio. Quincy rubbed his neck restlessly. Both glanced around and Aaron came over to greet them and open Lois' door.

The hazy afternoon was heavy with the threat of a coming summer storm, and Mercedes coughed with her first breath of the heat and humidity when her brother opened her door.

Aaron walked the ladies to the porch steps, but Quincy only nodded to acknowledge them and turned back to stare at the passage. Mercedes' heart sank. Zeke went to stand beside him, and Mercedes lingered on the porch steps for a few moments, clutching her bright sunflower-bedecked work tablet case against her blue linen sleeveless blouse.

Quincy squatted down in front of the passage. He pointed and said something to her brother. Her pulse quickened when Zeke knelt and put his hand to the ground, then motioned for Quincy to do the same. When Quincy obeyed, he jerked his head up to meet Zeke's eyes.

Mercedes ducked away to follow the others to the front door. Her brother was an Ellison. He sensed what she had, and he was leading Quincy to observe telltale signs that a force was active around them. Her next breath was a prayer for heaven's protection. Invisible battles were fought in unseen realms.

After Mercedes and Aaron inspected the house together, he offered to get the photos she needed in the kitchen. Grateful that he knew she could not bring herself to go there yet, she told him she would be with the other ladies in Doran's suite at the secluded side of the house.

Entering his room, she found Lois and Mary Lou looking through his desk and filing cabinet. Lois glanced up. "Oh, there you are. Do you mind starting in the closet? Maybe check Doran's jacket pockets, old wallets, and storage boxes? Mary Lou, if you'll unlock this steamer trunk, I'll search it next."

Mercedes could only stand still, her eyes wandering about the explorer's room. The décor and furnishings left no doubt who Doran Marlowe had been and what he liked.

Instinctively, her hand reached out to touch a well-traveled pith helmet perched on a stand on his large wooden dresser. She wondered what Doran looked like in it, then got her answer. Nearby, he was wearing it in an assortment of photos on location with various people.

Mary Lou came to stand by her and smiled at the photos. "See this one? That's a picture of us together once, when I was serving in Africa. In this larger one, we're in the middle with our Masai friends around us under the tree where we had worship services."

She pointed out other sentimental photos and objects on the dresser that her brother kept out to remind him of his adventures as a younger man. "And over here, on top of his chest of drawers, he still has a stack of his sketchbooks from various countries. Someday when you have time, I hope you'll come visit me and we'll look through them."

It overwhelmed Mercedes to have such a generous opportunity, and she promised she would schedule time to do that. Then she realized what was hanging on the wall behind the sketchbooks. "I can't believe it! A Khipu," she whispered, and stepped over for a closer look.

Mary Lou moved with her. "A fascinating tool that has stood the test of time. This is not a real one, of course, like in museums. Villagers who recorded the number of animals in their herds created and kept this. It amused them that Doran found it so intriguing, so they taught him how they counted and gave him this old one. They made a new one with the next year's inventory."

Aaron peeked in the door to say that Jansen Kirk had joined Quincy and Zeke outside. He was going out to see if they had any new information to share.

Mercedes remembered she should help Mary Lou instead of acting like a tourist, so she opened the double closet doors. She walked into the masculine smells of cedar and leather, and a faint exotic scent she imagined as being from a faraway place. For a few moments, she felt like an intruder. Her eyes roamed the clothing and accessories of a man who spent most of his life in the freedom of open places — dangerous, wild, faraway places.

There had been nothing pretentious about Doran Marlowe. His retirement had been recent, but he seemed not to have updated his wardrobe to the resort casual style so common in the Bluffton and Hilton Head area. Comfortable shirts, pants, and cargo style shorts in natural colors filled the hangers. All ranges of beige and olive-green drab were the rule, punctuated by a few shirts in white and sky blue. She mused he was most comfortable in the natural colors he spent his life in.

She reached a tentative hand to touch an aging leather travel pack that caught her eye. In her experience, what people put in a backpack, briefcase, or purse said a lot about who they are. This one was sturdy, meant to take a beating for years.

And it had. The random scratches across the brass latch were a testament to this. She suddenly wished she had known Doran and heard him tell his remarkable stories.

The latch needed oil, but after a brief struggle, she slid it open. It felt wrong to be investigating someone else's possessions, so she gingerly pulled open the worn leather flap. Inside, there were a few compartments, all of them buttoned up. The scent of tanned leather, musky sweat, and aging paper wafted up, tickling her nose.

She sneezed twice. From behind her in Doran's room, she heard Lois say, "Bless you!"

Mercedes had a mounting sense of expectation as she sat on the closet floor with the backpack. Fingering a loose button hanging by one strong thread, she lifted the flap of a large pocket. Inside, she found a bent wire pair of reading glasses, a stained, much-handled journal, an ink pen, a stub of a wooden pencil with no eraser left on the end, and a scratched magnifying glass with a carved ivory handle. And in the main compartment was a tattered letter-sized envelope and another folded, thick, business-sized envelope. Both had a foreign postmark that she thought she recognized.

The sensation of suspended time fell over Mercedes, and she fleetingly longed to hear about the impossible trails where this backpack traveled. The items inside were vital to the owner, and her imagination mingled with the photos on his dresser to create scenes where he wrote in the journal by firelight, wearing the wire reading glasses.

Sudden tears sprang to her eyes, and she sniffed. Oh, how narrowly she had missed a chance to know Doran Marlowe!

Did these communications contain some information Mary Lou wanted? She could not shake the feeling that these envelopes were clues that shed light on what had destroyed Doran.

Aaron's voice at the door to Doran's room gave her a start. It was time to face the garage and studio. Scooping up the scarred, slouchy leather of the backpack and closing the loose button, she left the closet.

"Mary Lou, I found this backpack, and it's not empty," she announced, plopping the pack onto a handmade patchwork quilt that was folded neatly on the bed. "I don't know if it's what you're looking for, but you should go through it soon, just in case."

Aaron's deep voice and lazy accent were soothing as he led the ladies outside across the veranda, asking them about the household records Mary Lou had in Doran's room. It had been decades since she had managed a household. The places where she spent her life had simple cultures that survived from day to day, so the network of bills and service providers that her brother paid monthly was dizzying for her.

So intense was Mercedes' apprehension at going into the garage studio that she barely paid attention to the discussion.

Her friends had not seen the painting in Doran Marlowe's studio, seen the horrified expression on his face, or heard the other-worldly buzzing overhead. Only her concern for her brother and her fiancé made her go there now, despite her curiosity about the other covered paintings on easels or stored away there.

Then they heard a woman's shrill voice from the driveway. Mercedes' group slowed near the veranda steps before descending them to the yard.

"Your obsession with this place and the dead man is sick, Jansen! The old guy just croaked, okay? It happens. Is this all an excuse to avoid me?"

Mercedes rested her hand lightly on the verandah railing. Dr. Jansen Kirk was here, in jogging attire, standing beside an expensive convertible sports car. A dark-haired driver with an angry attitude had pulled up along the edge of the side road at Marlowe House. The cut-out sections on the shoulders of the pretty blouse she wore revealed slices of her skin getting pink in the sun.

Jansen stood with his arms crossed, talking to the woman over the purr of the engine from the passenger door side. "You're the one with an obsession, out here stalking me," he said flatly. "I jog this route every day when I vacation here, and I saw these guys out looking around. I stopped to see if I could help."

Mercedes dragged her eyes away from the private argument to find her brother and Quincy, who waited by the door to the garage for Aaron and her group. The angry brunette blurted, "I don't think so. She's the attraction! What, are blondes the summer flavor of the week now, Jansen?"

The doctor jerked his head around and saw Mercedes, who flushed with more than the heat of the day. She clutched her computer tablet close and walked purposefully toward the others. Jansen turned and leaned with both hands on the side of the convertible. His words were inaudible, but no one missed his steely tone. Then he pointed sternly toward the main road.

The young woman pulled expensive sunglasses down to her face and tossed her head. Her voice was hard. "Pick me up on time for the gala at the Bluffs tonight or never call me again!"

The convertible jerked onto the road and Jansen spun on his heel to join the others. He glowered, and his jaw muscles worked in tension as he quickly caught up with Mercedes and lightly took her arm. "I am so sorry," he murmured, leaning his head down close to hers.

Her angry flush was cooling as they reached the rest of the group. But the jealous woman's insult had rattled her. With a nod to convey that she accepted his apology, she gently tried to pull her arm away. But his grip tightened. Startled, she glanced up at his profile while he addressed everyone.

"I apologize to you all for that scene, and especially to Miss Marlowe and to Miss Ellison. It was unforgiveable the way my friend spoke of Doran, and the insult about Mercedes couldn't have happened at a worse time. I know better than anyone what we're getting ready to do is hard for her, since I was here that day." He glanced down at her and gave her elbow a reassuring squeeze.

Aaron took the keys from Mary Lou and worked the lock on the door. Mercedes quickly met her brother's eyes and noted his raised brows. She glanced at Quincy, but he was busy studying Jansen.

Her heart fell. Jansen had been outside talking to Aaron, Zeke, and Quincy for the last twenty minutes. Quincy had failed to mention that Mercedes was his fiancée.

She wiped sweat from her brow with the back of her free hand, fluffing her damp bangs and struggling with a spark of anger. Jansen was right. She dreaded going back into the scene of Doran's death. And the one person she wanted by her side was coolly walking through the now-open door without looking back.

She followed Jansen's lead and took what comfort she could in his well-meaning hold on her arm. He had witnessed the discovery of Doran Marlowe's body, but he could not yet grasp her perspective of the situation. She silently breathed a prayer for the safety of her group of friends.

Chapter 7

Mercedes held her breath, but nothing unexpected happened when she and her escort followed the rest of their group into the spacious, barn-like interior of Doran Marlowe's art studio. The air-conditioned coolness was a welcome relief, and light flooded in from well-placed windows and skylights. Everyone stood still at first after walking in, looking around in the hushed silence, getting their bearings. The space was unremarkable at first glance and had a lingering odor of art gesso and cleaning solutions.

Aaron looked back. "Mercedes, what do you need for your records? Photos and measurements?"

Mercedes felt uneasy and warily scanned the rafters of the building for the sound she had heard the last time she was there. The sooner she got what she needed for Mary Lou's paperwork, the sooner she could get Zeke and Quincy out of this place.

Nodding to Aaron, she said, "Yes, thank you, and I'd appreciate your suggestions. Mary Lou could change course and turn this space into a showcase of Doran's collections, stories, and paintings, setting special event dates to invite the public. Otherwise, she should consider the low upkeep of converting the building back into a garage with parking space for her renting guests."

Mary Lou's voice wavered as she said, "I need common sense advice about how to, or whether, to move forward with Doran's plans for the property. I don't see how I can do it without him, and I'm uncertain he would want me to."

Lois patted her arm and said, "We'll help. Let's start looking around over at the far side."

Mercedes saw her chance to pull away from Jansen. He easily let her arm slide from his as she took her work tablet to Aaron. "Use this for photos, just like in the kitchen of the main house. Thank you so much for helping me."

Quincy silently studied the studio space and Mercedes knew what was on his mind. He stood with hands on hips, looking at random artifacts stored on shelves and connecting them to places he knew about. Especially any that hinted at a certain area of South America.

Jansen stepped over to speak to Zeke. "Since you're a doctor, I want to ask you about something I saw the day we found the body. In all my days of internship and practice, I've never heard of it."

Zeke studied Jansen's face and found an honest appeal for a professional opinion. "Is this about the expression on Mr. Marlowe's face?"

Jansen sighed with relief and swiped a hand over his forehead. Zeke said, "I heard about it. Mercedes is my little sister."

After he blinked in surprise, Jansen grinned wryly. "I don't know how I missed the family resemblance. She never mentioned having a brother who was a doctor."

He glanced at Mercedes as they spoke. "In fact, she was shaky and evasive. It was upsetting for her, the EMT, and me. The officers were predictably stone-faced about it. Have you ever seen anything like we described?"

"Yes, but only in the mission field and on archaeology dig sites," Zeke answered. "Mercedes has, too. That's what shook her up so much. It doesn't fit in small towns in America, and Doran's death will be called a heart attack or stroke. There will be no satisfying explanation for his expression. It's not something you can talk to anyone in the medical field or law enforcement about, either, because I've tried, and they won't accept the obvious. And the obvious is why I'm here right now."

Jansen ventured, "Are the expressions you've seen before caused by a hallucinogen?"

They all turned to Quincy's voice. "No. It was a supernatural encounter."

Mercedes, Zeke, and Jansen watched as Quincy let the drape over a covered painting slide to the studio floor with a soft rustle. For a few moments, they all stared at the scene Doran Marlowe worked on the night he died. Quincy pointed to certain places in it from the standpoint of an archaeologist.

He turned to Mercedes with a new respect in his eyes. "When you described this to me on the phone the day you found Doran, I had a vague idea of it from the dig site. But this—"

He blew out his breath and ran his hands over his face. "This is powerful. I don't know what inspired him to record it, but he knew the reality of this ritual. I understand why you were so disturbed and what an impact it would have to stumble on this scene."

Her voice cracked, then steadied. "I avoid looking at the underground part since I glimpsed what is happening. But overall, Doran believed two realms exist, real time, like the 'thin places,' or portals. One is invisible, but both are real."

Her voice grew stronger, and she waved a hand to show the painting. "He painted the underground tunnel or abyss to be like hell, or worse, and the grotesque creatures who are torturing humans or human souls are like the images of pagan gods found around the globe—part human, part animal, part male, part female, but altogether totally unnatural mixes of species and genders, as if to subvert God's order of creation in Genesis."

She stepped closer and pointed to the upper half. "See how the humans are apparently oblivious to what's happening under their feet? Doran believed the idol deceived the worshippers who were sacrificing fellow humans to meet the demands of their patron god. They didn't grasp the truth about the entity that the idol represented. It is not their earthly benefactor, nor will it grant them a good afterlife. They assume that they have satisfied the demands of their god for the time being and that they will receive a reward for it."

Now she pointed to other areas on the canvas. "See the blood color streaked through the painting, in the sky, on the altar and ground, and spilling the cup? Like most pagan gods, this one is predictable. It demanded blood. The worshipers carve an idol and invite the evil entity to inhabit it through the mouth-opening rituals. They willingly bind themselves to serve it."

Coming another step closer, Mercedes pointed to the being concealing itself behind the idol. She had to clear her throat when her voice cracked again. "This is where Doran stopped. See?"

Her heart pounded and her voice dropped to just above a whisper. "Or maybe I'm the only one who notices. This blurred, hideous—thing—crouching behind that statue, through the portal, is holding a glowing orb, stirring it with his claw as he exercises supernatural power over the humans."

"I see it," said Quincy. "And you're right, that's the only unfinished part of the painting."

He squinted and leaned closer. "Doran saved that for the end. He tried to paint what the being looks like, from descriptions, and somehow, it brought on the horror that froze on his face."

Jansen drew a quick breath, but Mercedes heard something else. Her nerves felt electrified and with a sharp look up, she tried to see where the growing, angry buzzing sound came from.

She gasped as Zeke jerked her to him and shouted to Quincy to run. Shoving Mercedes against Jansen, he pushed them both back.

Dazed, Mercedes wondered when the crashing sounds would end, and whether Quincy dove out of danger in time. Aaron called out a warning. Lois cried out to Mercedes from a distance, and Mary Lou wailed in dismay.

But the main thought in Mercedes' mind was that she had not been the only one who heard the buzzing sound. Her brother did!

The mayhem in the garage studio was the stuff of nightmares, but Mercedes knew she was living through it. This was no movie. A passing sense of desperation swept over her as she absently rubbed her forearm.

Still stunned and uncertain if she was in danger, Mercedes crawled to sit up on the stack of musty canvas drop cloths she had stumbled on when her brother shoved her out of harm's way. Time passed in slow motion, but it could only have been seconds before Jansen righted himself and squatted down to check her injuries.

Dazed, she let him take her arm to examine where it hurt, and he told her to expect a bruise. Then he swiftly looked for any serious problems and found none.

In a rush, she came to herself and gripped his arm. "Jansen, quick! Find Quincy! I'll check on Zeke."

He nodded and turned to pick his way carefully in the direction of where Quincy had been. Mercedes reached for her brother, who groaned as he raised up on his elbows. Glass and other debris splintered as Aaron made his way to Zeke's feet.

"Hold on! Wait just a minute there, Zeke," he drawled. "Let me lift this broken easel off your leg."

There was a general confusion of Lois and Mary Lou's warnings to everyone about the damage. Mercedes half-smiled weakly at her brother. "You're still my superhero after all these years. And you've been holding out on me, acting like you don't have the Ellison instincts. You heard the buzzing and reacted before I did."

With a spontaneous grin, he quipped, "And you're still cute after all these years, but comin' to your rescue ain't as simple as it used to be. Aww!" he yelped. "What in the world?"

He craned his neck to see Aaron behind him. The older man hushed him and said, "Hang on, I'll help you get turned over and see if you can walk. You got yourself a nasty bruise comin' up already on your lower leg here, near your ankle. Not a lot of muscle there to cushion that smash up from the easel. That's a heavy one."

As Aaron and Mercedes helped him, Zeke asked about Quincy. "Jansen is with him. I'm going over to check on him now."

Zeke waved her off. "Go on, Aaron can get me up from here, and we'll find the fuse box to turn off the electricity to the studio lights. What a mess!"

Indeed, what a mess, in more ways than one, thought Mercedes as she stood and saw the extent of the damage done. A light fixture that fell from the ceiling connected wiring and chains to several more, one of which crashed to the ground with the first and the other one hung by a chain. It still swayed, the bulb flickering. An explosion of easels, shelves, and other art supplies lay strewn about.

Twenty feet away, Quincy was sitting propped up against the studio wall, answering Jansen's questions. Lois and Mary Lou were nearby, cleaning up scattered items that had fallen off a shelf so no one would trip over them.

Deciding on the easiest path through the chaos, Mercedes picked her way to Quincy and used her sandals to brush away debris so she could kneel beside him. Under his tousled dark hair was a reddish lump, and he winced as Jansen prodded around his left shoulder.

Grimly, she asked, "How is he, Doctor Kirk?"

"He's extremely lucky, like the rest of us. I need to get him in the house to disinfect some cuts on the back of his legs, but I removed the shards. He needs no stitches. But he needs ice on that bump on the head. That plastic pail full of paint brushes glanced off his face, just missing his eye, and he crashed into the shelving and bruised his shoulder. I recommend something for pain, since he'll have a headache and an aching shoulder."

Quincy reached for her hand and said softly, "You heard the man. I'm fine. Don't look so miserable. This isn't your fault."

Mercedes squeezed her eyes tight against tears, but they escaped. She sniffed and swiped at the ones that rolled down her face.

Jansen snorted. "Of course, it's not her fault. That's ridiculous! The lighting in here is old, it was a matter of time before something like this happened."

Mercedes wiped another stray tear away and gulped. Slowly, his expression sobered. "Why in the world would you believe this has anything to do with you?"

He turned to Quincy. "Does she think what happened to her in the house yesterday is behind this, like a warning or a bogey man after her?"

"Not after her. After me, or me and her brother," replied Quincy, squeezing her hand again.

Jansen's expression was incredulous as Mary Lou and Lois gathered around them. Aaron came over, with Zeke limping and leaning on him. Jansen offered his hand to help Quincy, who swayed when he got up, then closed his eyes.

"Woah, there," warned Jansen, and both he and Mercedes reached out to steady Quincy. "Take it easy a couple of days to get over that bump on the head."

"Shouldn't I call for help?" asked Mary Lou. Her face was tense with concern.

"No cause," Zeke said. "We aren't seriously injured. Let's get everyone in the house for first aid and go from there with our next step."

Aaron drawled, "Yeah, let's get outta here. We need to tend to the wounded and feed the hungry. I'll call some friends from church later to get help to clean up this mess."

"Mess? This isn't a mess, it's a disaster!" cried Mary Lou. "It's a miracle everyone is okay!"

"Then we've seen a miracle," Lois said, sounding like her usual practical self. "It's not the first time for most of us."

Jansen let Quincy lean on Mercedes and Lois while he hurried to open and hold the studio door. But he did a double take as he held the knob. "Mary Lou! Mary Lou, come here!"

The older woman rushed to his side. "What is it? Is anything wrong?"

"I just—" he halted as he pointed out to the curb across the street. "He was here a minute ago! The same man the officer and I saw watching your house."

He left her holding the door for Aaron to help Zeke through and ran out into the driveway parking area. Then he ran to the edge of the side road, turning all around. When the others were out the door, Mary Lou followed him, shading her eyes against the bright sunshine. The rest of the group limped onto the verandah.

Jansen shook his head, then lifted his hands in surrender and went to walk with Mary Lou to the house. "Unless I'm imagining things, I saw the same man, in the same clothes. I hoped you would tell me if it's your friend."

Mary Lou took his offered arm for help on the verandah stairs. With a teasing smile, she said, "You mean the friend that keeps coming to my mind? I thought you didn't believe me, Doctor Kirk."

The young doctor shook his head and chuckled. "A lot has happened since I doubted you, Miss Marlowe."

"I haven't been to the grocery store in a few days," said Mary Lou as she put first aid supplies on the generous-sized sofa table. "I have some herbal teas, coffee, bottled water, and lemons to make up some fresh lemonade, if anyone wants some."

Aaron looked up from soaking cotton squares with peroxide. "I'll take some lemonade if it's not much trouble, and we'll get up an order for takeout or delivery. We've got a lot to talk about."

"Mary Lou, we need to finish in Doran's room to help you with the funeral," Lois added, rising to her feet. "What does everyone else want to drink? Mary Lou, where are those menus I saw in your kitchen?"

"Ouch!" yelped Quincy as Aaron dabbed at the cuts on the back of his legs. Looking around, he said, "Mercedes, do you mind taking over? Aaron still thinks he's hammering nails on a construction site."

Smirking, Aaron told him to stop whining, and Quincy pointed out where his wound was bleeding again from the rough nursing. Over on the sofa, Zeke spoke through clenched teeth as Jansen probed the bruise on his leg. "Yikes, take it easy!"

"Give me a break, you know the drill," quipped Jansen. "If we get that swelling down, you can limp on your own. Might have to miss a couple of days' work. I'll get ice from Mary Lou."

Mercedes picked up the cotton squares and asked Quincy to lie down on his stomach on the floor so she could reach his cuts easier. He sighed and gingerly got on the cool hardwoods, favoring his shoulder.

When only Mercedes, Zeke, and Quincy remained in the living room, she kept her voice low and said, "Look at both of you. What if we hadn't heard the buzzing, Zeke? What will we tell Mom and Dad? Dad sensed something would happen to you, and it did."

Zeke sighed and mumbled something she could not hear. She lightly swathed the soft cotton squares over cuts on the back on Quincy's legs, and one snagged. "Oh, no," she muttered.

"Easy! That one stings," Quincy said tightly.

Mercedes looked over at her brother. "Zeke, I think there's something sharp here that Jansen missed."

He leaned up on his elbow and peered across the table at the first aid supplies. "Grab those tweezers and wipe them to be sure they're disinfected. She's gotta get that out, Quincy."

"I can go find Jansen," Mercedes said. "Or Quincy can come stand over there on the sofa and you can do it."

But Quincy grabbed her arm. "No, it's okay. Just do the best you can."

Zeke teased, "He knows you come from a long line of physicians, Mercedes. And your name means 'mercy,' which Jansen and I aren't likely to have for him."

"It's great to know that if she messes up, there are two unmerciful doctors in the house itching to get to me," growled Quincy.

Zeke laughed and Mercedes grinned, settling into a position to see the debris on Quincy's leg. Jansen came in with his arms full of ice packs, pain relievers, and water bottles, stopping short at the sight of Mercedes.

"It's okay, Jansen. They'll be married soon," Zeke joked. "She wanted you to get some debris out of that wound, but he thinks his chances are better with her than with you or me."

"Oh," Jansen said, setting down the supplies and handing an ice pack to Zeke. "Okay. Well, here, Mercedes, at least let me get a flashlight on that cut so you can see better."

Mercedes waited on the extra light and took a deep breath before easing the tweezers close to the wound. "It's something dark and shiny. I think I've got it."

By the time Quincy winced, she was done. Close beside her, Jansen remarked it looked like a sliver of metal and praised her precision. As she swathed the wound again with cotton, he was handing out pain relievers and Aaron was taking orders for dinner.

Chapter 8

Mary Lou's living room was quiet after the food delivery arrived. Everyone was reluctant to talk after Aaron took the containers out to the trash cans and came back, wiping sweat from his forehead. "Looks like a storm is brewing," he rasped.

Lois checked the weather app on her phone. "The 'real feel' is at 105 right now with a good chance for a storm tonight. That would cool things off. And it looks like there could be pop-up storms the rest of the week."

Jansen cleared his throat and leaned forward, clasping his hands together and resting them on his knees. "I'll risk a storm, help clean the studio, and cancel a date if someone will please explain to me what happened in the studio today. Officer Cordera said things we may not think are relevant could be important."

Mercedes held an ice pack to the tender bruise on her arm and exchanged a meaningful glance with Quincy, who pressed another pack to the lump on his forehead. Zeke shifted his elevated leg in Mary Lou's recliner and replied, "If it's with the young lady in the convertible, cancel that date, regardless. You should reconsider your curiosity about all this. I'm not being flippant when I warn you that if we tell you the truth, it will change your life. This will be a point of no return."

Jansen's eyes narrowed. "I've been on a trail of those points of no return since the day I followed your sister to this house."

Zeke guffawed and glanced at Mercedes, who closed her eyes and sighed. He said, "Yeah, many people start that way. It's only the beginning."

He shifted his injured leg again and looked back at Jansen. "But if you really want to go down this road, I'll talk about it if you'll do something for me. I need photographs of the paintings that Doran covered up. I think they're important."

Jansen scowled and nodded. "Will the paintings help explain what's going on?"

"I don't know. Are you willing to go back and photograph the paintings and text the photos to me?"

The young doctor spread his hands. "Well—sure. What do you expect to see?"

This time, Quincy answered. "We're interested in whether Doran Marlowe depicted one of the elaborate rituals of divination and human sacrifice the Inca elite practiced. I'd like to know which god he was trying to paint when he died. The Inca weren't a civilization as we think, they were the elite governors of an empire. They embraced a pantheon of gods, animism, and fetishism, but they also tolerated the gods of the villagers they ruled so harshly."

Jansen stared at him in doubt. "You've got a slight British accent, and it sounds like you've traveled to South America. I take it from your answer, and the analysis of the painting a while ago, that you're in the history field?"

Zeke laughed outright and glanced at Quincy, whose usual quick grin was back. Zeke said, "Quincy has a British father who got swept off his feet and out of his family's expectations when he married an American woman. He mostly grew up on archaeology dig sites all over the world, so his, and his father's, combined experience, important discoveries, research, published scholarship, connections, and expertise are in high demand in history circles like archaeology and antiquities. He's been in, or in search of, lost cities, lost civilizations, lost treasures, and legendary creatures. Quincy's an authority on many topics, including some blurry fringe ones he has shared little about publicly. And his trademark is to analyze everything through the lens of a biblical worldview. That's important because we've found that it's the only way any of it makes any sense."

Quincy grinned at Jansen. "Right now, I'm just a humble consultant with antiquities, museums, and archaeology digs. My fiancé keeps me busy with those fringe interests—like what we're investigating right now."

Jansen studied him, then nodded. "Okay, so Mercedes *is* involved in this, as I suspected. And if you're a consultant on these topics, you're an expert."

Quincy shrugged, and Jansen sat back in his seat in resignation. "Let's say you're right about what's on those canvases. That you're right about Doran's dark subject. Those paintings are inanimate objects and didn't bring down the lights today. Not even the one he was working on could do that, as disturbing as it was."

Mary Lou suddenly gripped the arms of her chair and spoke up. "When I found my brother, I was so shocked I noticed nothing else. What was disturbing about the painting he was working on? Why has he covered his paintings lately?"

Quincy set aside the ice pack he'd been holding on his head and leaned forward. His voice was soft while his intense blue eyes held those of the older woman. "We aren't sure why he was covering them, Miss Marlowe. I hoped you might know. The scene he was working on couldn't be something he witnessed in his travels, because the civilization who once practiced human sacrifice no longer existed. I'm not saying it doesn't happen, but it's in hidden places. Maybe he studied about it or was told stories by locals. I'm interested in his audience for that painting. Did he mention any private commissions?"

Puzzled, Mary Lou sat considering this. "Doran only paints—painted—landscapes, unusual places he saw, and sometimes, the everyday life of tribes and villages he made friends in. He really loved to paint creation. If he had a commission for some historical subject, he said nothing about it. I have seen little of Doran lately. He was in his studio until all hours, and I was busy settling into the house and getting to know our rental guests."

Knitting her graying brows, she added, "I did notice that he penciled the word 'deadline' on a date on the wall calendar we use, and for our boarding guests to mark dates when they will be traveling. I believe it's for about a week from now."

"Mary Lou, we didn't finish searching through things in his room," said Lois. "Let's look for any clues about that deadline."

"That's a good place to start," Mercedes said, scooting up to the edge of her seat. "What about that bookbag I found in the closet? It has some correspondence and journals in it. I thought Mary Lou should be the one to open them."

"Woah, hold on, Mercedes, you're not getting out of here so easy," Jansen said, leaning forward again in his chair and holding out his arm as if to hold her back. "You're a part of all this and you haven't explained your role." He pointed to the kitchen hallway. "For a start, why did Officer Cordero act like a hound dog on the scent when he recognized your name? Second, what happened here yesterday, and how does it tie in with today's incident? And third, why did Quincy tell you all this isn't your fault?"

Mercedes settled back into her chair. "I need to rearrange the order of your questions and begin with the background for what happened yesterday. When I was seventeen, my family went to work for a few weeks on a dig site in Peru with Quincy's family. I hate to go to dig sites where ancient civilizations worshiped, because chilling artifacts and evidence turns up. But I never missed a chance to spend time with Quincy."

She glanced at Quincy and half-smiled before turning a somber look to Jansen. "One day, I worked with some women and teens walking past gloomy caves. They gestured to keep a certain distance from the spirits. Most of the niches for idols were empty, but in others, someone had carved hideous creatures directly into the rock. Locals believed one cave was a portal of sorts to another realm, where spirits can have access to the earth."

She knit her fingers together, then stopped and looked up to meet Jansen's eyes. "What happened is difficult to describe. I felt a blast of air, or wind, and I had a sense of being blocked from taking another step. Then came a vivid impression of being threatened by a presence I can't explain, and it had an awful loathing of me. Shocked and overwhelmed, I instantly cried out to Jesus for protection from His enemy. The darkness became smoke and fled, or was driven, back into a cave."

Mary Lou stifled a groan, and her hand flew to cover her mouth. Her eyes were wide with recognition.

Mercedes bit her lip, then said, "I guess I fainted, because the next thing I remember is the locals helping me rise from the ground. A few other people around me were being helped up, too, and children were gathering the things in our spilled baskets for us. Someone went for my parents and Quincy's father, and the supervisor who oversaw the dig. They had the doctor check for any injuries and then they questioned the group of us separately about what happened. Our stories were mostly the same as of the witnesses who came to help us get up. The superstitious locals named and blamed an ancient god."

With a glance at her brother for encouragement, she cleared her throat and continued her story. "The only one with a different account of what happened was me. I had heard, or had an impression of, or had totally imagined, a threat not to follow my family's path. The cost would be the safety of those I love."

Jansen stared blankly, then scratched his head. "What does that even mean about your 'family's path'?"

Seeing his sister hesitate, Zeke spoke again. "Now we can answer your first question. For generations, some of the Ellisons sense stranger things than normal people see. But we claim no abilities and don't control when it happens. We don't understand, nor do we look for those times to occur. To be frank, Jansen, we aren't crazy about it. That brings us to what you want to know about the incident in the studio today. When I first arrived, Quincy was here, outside, looking at the connecting passage. I don't know why, so just call it a hunch, but I put my hand to the ground. I asked him if he felt the vibration, like energy. And he did."

He waved his hand as if brushing an idea aside. "Sure, maybe we're close to a buried power line or something. I don't know. But admit it, just the fact that it even came to my attention is weird. See, my sister wasn't the only one who felt something was off in the studio and heard the buzzing. We both knew it wasn't just the wiring or a bulb. I reacted before she did to get her and Quincy away from that painting, and as you saw, it now has a lot of damage."

"And I heard the buzzing sound the day we found Doran," Mercedes said soberly. "You were there and noticed nothing. I felt so disturbed because I knew what it was and couldn't explain it to anyone who would understand. All I could think of was to get away from here."

She shifted in her chair and chose her next words carefully. "I believe I felt the same presence, and blocked path, that I encountered in Peru. Something is still connecting my life to the incident that happened at the Inca dig site."

"This happened yesterday while you were here, at my house?" asked Mary Lou. "I have seen this kind of thing many times, on the mission field."

"Yes," Mercedes said. "It was while you were resting. Lois and Jansen saw it, too, and Lois heard a sound, as I did. I had hoped not to tell you, but I really don't want you to stay alone. Please wait until we finish this. Let's get that passageway to the garage cleared out. You sense something is wrong with it. That's why you closed it off and hung a cross on the door."

Mary Lou nodded and whispered, "Of course. I should have known."

"And that's not all," Zeke said. "My sister has a journal from our Great-Great Grand Aunt Mercedes, who recorded an eerily similar encounter. She even sketched the cave entrance, and it's a lot like the one we saw in Peru, though we don't know if it's the same location. If it's really a thin place or portal, as the spirits told local natives, it could open to other locations in the world. Anyway, our aunt heard the same message my sister got, and later, her husband died."

Jansen stared at them with obvious skepticism. He forced a humorless chuckle. "Zeke, come on. You're a man of science."

Zeke nodded. "Yes, I am, and a man of faith. Every day, I see something I can't explain. Don't you?"

He reached into his shorts pocket. "Here, key in your number to my phone and I'll send you mine. If you're willing, Quincy and I will share with you why our careers are not incompatible with what you witnessed today in the studio. Let's help Mary Lou find some tangible evidence about Doran's motivation for his painting, and I'll stick around a few days to be with my sister and Quincy. Our family has questions and loose ends to tie up about all this. Then we can have lunch and talk."

Hesitantly, Jansen reached for the cell phone Zeke was offering him. But he turned back to Mercedes.

"When Officer Cordera met you here, then kept watching your reactions to the scene—is that what you mean about your family's 'path'? After his instant recognition and respect for you, I read several news reports online mentioning your name this summer. While the circumstances weren't typical, the reports didn't link you to paranormal activity."

Mercedes flinched and groaned. "I don't want to be associated with that description, and authorities don't want to report anything supernatural. Even if the evidence makes better sense in a spiritual perspective, the law enforcement reports are always written in worldly terms."

With meaningful glances at Zeke and Quincy, she added, "We try to stick to only facts people will accept when we are witnesses to these events. But investigators often know there's more to the story, and they tell each other. That's why Officer Cordera watched me."

"And for the record, Peru is crawling with things that have no natural explanation," Quincy said. He gave a nod to Mary Lou. "Miss Marlowe can tell you true stories you'll never forget. I was hesitant when my parents invited the Ellisons to our dig site at the time Mercedes had her strange encounter. Give us a chance at credibility by going online, looking into the rituals of the Incas, and for modern news, you'll find more reports and eyewitness videos than you can watch about things that defy any logical explanation."

Aaron's phone rang, bringing them all back to their own situation. He answered and gave someone Mary Lou's address, then thanked them for their help. After hanging up, he said friends would arrive shortly to help clean up the garage.

Aaron's group from church wore safety goggles, leather gloves, and work boots as they cleaned up the mess in the garage studio, and Jansen went to find and photograph the paintings Zeke requested. With each one, he grew more perplexed.

He re-covered the last canvas, then pursed his lips, wondering at the inscription Doran Marlowe had noted in the back corner on the wood of the stretched canvas frame. He stashed this series of paintings in a corner so Aaron and Lois' pastor and church friends would not come across them. His idea of Christians was that they attended churches like club members, shunning the reality of the world and escaping to the narrowmindedness of their own ideology.

Yet, his new acquaintances were nothing like that. And as he looked at the busy church members, they were a mixed bag. Two wore uniform work shirts with local business logos, and two more wore designer golf polos. A tanned young man who might be a college student wore a tee shirt advertising a local kayak adventure shop.

He wished he could find something to criticize, but these men had a special accord and sweet camaraderie. An unexpected stab of longing ran him through, and he let it pass. But he knew the yearning sensation had left him changed.

The cleaning team must wonder what had caused the lights to suddenly buzz and come down like this. He was uncertain what Aaron had told them, or if they understood how narrowly Quincy, Zeke, and Mercedes had come to serious injuries. What would they think of the explanations and stories he heard an hour ago?

Mary Lou Marlowe brought Zeke an old set of crutches and a carved walking cane from a closet, leaning them by the sofa, where he reclined with his foot up. Quincy was in her recliner, holding a small ice pack over a lump on his forehead. Mercedes worked on her tablet with the photos she and Aaron had taken of the house.

She left the room and was soon back with her brother's travel-worn backpack. "Let's explore this where we all can see it," she announced, and she knelt by the coffee table.

Mercedes came to sit beside her, and Lois drew up a chair as close as she could. An air of excitement and anticipation fell over the group as she laid the heavy pack on the table. "When everything is out, I'll open any envelopes and journals."

"Let's pray over it first," Quincy suggested, as he sat up and laid his limp ice pack down. "This is a connection with your brother, and it may reveal a side of him you didn't know. It sounds like you spent most of your life apart, in remote places. You didn't hear from him often, did you?"

The older woman swallowed hard, then shook her head sadly. "We tried to keep in touch, but letters would get delayed, and we'd get several at once. He got a cellphone a few years ago for emergencies because more villages had satellite services, but he needed special equipment to keep it charged. That meant more weight in his backpack. Now and then, he'd call the main office to find out if they could reach me, and we'd get to hear each other's voices."

Her smile was tremulous. "He said he'd get me one and teach me to use it when I came home. It was supposed to be a comfort to me as I started driving again, running errands, so I could call and ask him things. Maybe Lois can teach me to use his now."

"Has anyone called him?" Zeke asked.

"Why, I—I haven't even thought about that. It's on his dresser, in his room, but it's not on. We have this home phone, and it's all I use. I've not heard or seen him use the other one since I came back. Few people had that number."

Zeke said, "We'll try it later. You'll need a password to unlock it. One thing at a time. Let's pray for wisdom, discernment, and comfort about what we find in the backpack and thank Jesus for the blessing your brother was to you while you were together in this life."

Jansen opened the front door and froze to see the group gathered and linking hands around the sofa table. "Oh, I'm sorry. Am I interrupting?"

Lois smiled and welcomed him in. "Not at all. We're going to pray together before opening Doran's old backpack. If you're staying longer, won't you join us?"

The young doctor slowly closed the door behind him, then hesitated. "Is something wrong with the bag?"

Zeke chuckled. "After what happened today, we're not taking any chances. No tellin' where it's been!"

Jansen laughed outright along with them, and Lois said, "We know this sounds strange to most people, but we ask Jesus for guidance and answers when we can't see what to do next. This backpack is a bittersweet connection for Mary Lou with her brother. Opening it is part of the healing process, of remembering, letting go, and moving on. We're also searching for clues about what Doran's deadline is for, whether we can meet his obligation, and if he left behind anything that will explain what happened to him."

Jansen walked in and took a seat nearby. "I'll stay. Thanks for inviting me to join you."

Mercedes recognized the scent of tanned leather and aging paper when Mary Lou slid the scratched brass latch open on Doran's bag. And like she had done, Mary Lou hesitated before opening the heavy outer flap to reveal compartments that were buttoned up.

The open pack tipped against the table. Mary Lou fingered the loose button on a large outside pocket, smiling sadly at the neglected repair, and lifted the flap.

Almost reverently, she pulled out a bent wire pair of reading glasses and a magnifying glass with a lovely ivory handle carved to look like a high waterfall. The next items in the pocket were an ink pen, a battered pencil stub that needed sharpening and an eraser, and a bound journal or notebook stained with handling.

Mary Lou pulled other items from other pockets, including a multi-function pocketknife, a compass, matches, and personal care items. "It looks like Doran has already removed most of what he carried," she observed.

Now that the pockets were empty, Mercedes waited anxiously to see what Mary Lou would pull out of the slouching bag. The first item was the tattered letter-sized envelope, and the next was the thick, folded manila envelope. Doran had opened both and tucked them back inside.

Mary Lou scowled at the foreign postmarks before handing the envelopes to Quincy. "What do you make of these?"

Quincy's brows shot up and he let out a low whistle. Zeke leaned in closer to see what he held. Then their startled eyes met over the envelopes.

Quincy turned the envelopes over and studied the writing again. He cleared his throat and said, "Doran was corresponding with people who are notoriously difficult to work with. For archaeology and antiquities in South America, the government controls all narratives, no matter if the evidence supports them or what the tribes know. Most will tell you the worst is Peru."

He ran his hands over the envelopes as he spoke and seemed to weigh them in his palms. Mercedes felt a pang of—what? He looked so much in his element that she almost wished he was back in the field again, doing what he loved, solving puzzles and weaving together the tapestry of history.

Looking up, he said, "Mary Lou, will you open these? There may be clues inside. And I admit, I'm eager to see if Doran dealt with the same officials and roadblocks I ran into."

Mary Lou nodded and her hand trembled as she reached for the envelopes Quincy held out. She pulled on a pair of reading glasses and opened the smaller envelope. Two letters came out. After scanning the first page, she said, "This one is from a contact Doran had. He was working with him to turn in any artifacts he stumbled on while exploring, and to give locations for any sites he found that were off the beaten track. But another contact was interested in including one item in a documentary, so Doran asked permission to take it out of the country."

She paused and ran her eyes over the rest of the letter. "This contact made a mistake about an item, thinking it was a household or village idol of some sort carved by a tribesman. As the agency came across the information later to file in their records, a researcher working with material on an excavation site in Piquillacta noticed that this was an item of importance and needed to be returned to be studied more. It ends with an apology for the mistake and the inconvenience and says an official envelope will follow. They will send instructions about how and where he is to meet someone to deliver the artifact."

She picked up the large manila envelope. "This might be the information he mentioned."

Anticipation was thick as everyone leaned closer. Mary Lou slid out a crisp, official looking letter and peered at it through her reading glasses. "This is the arrangement to meet Doran and get an item of historic importance that he's been contacted about. I'll check the calendar to be sure, but I believe it's the date he scribbled in as his deadline."

Quincy was squirmy in his seat, keeping his eyes on Mary Lou. "Does the agency name the item?"

"No," she murmured, looking over the letter again.

Quincy and Zeke looked at one another and spoke the same words almost at once. "It's Wari."

"Oh, man," Quincy's voice trailed off. He absently lifted his hand to rake back his hair and bumped it against the small lump on his forehead. Gasping, he winced.

Mercedes paled and rubbed her hands over her upper arms as if to ward off a sudden chill. Jansen looked around at the group. "Who's Wari?"

"It's not a person, it's a culture that existed about seven hundred years before the Inca," Quincy replied. "We know little about them, but we link them to the excavation at Piquillacta. The name translates as 'flea place' and it's about twelve miles from Cusco, Peru. The culture dates from about 600-1000 A.D. They left no written records we've found, and wherever they conquered other people, they imposed their language, gods, and culture on them, ending the local oral traditions. But the climate preserved items in the tombs of their elite citizens, so we have some idea of their skill in ceramics and textile design."

"Most of the ones I've seen are depictions of grotesque faces," Mercedes said soberly. "Some even look like today's emojis on our phones. I only realized that just now and may never use a smiley face in my texts again."

Zeke grinned wryly. "Great, now you've ruined emojis for me. I never noticed that before, either."

"There's a lot represented in those faces, if we only had written records to decipher them," Quincy said. "We think the equivalent of shamans are among them, so they're likely messages to or from their spirit gods."

Jansen stood up and wiped his hands over his face. Then he set his hands on his hips and looked around at the others. "What a day. So, Doran brought back some sort of curiosity he collected from his travels and was going to let someone else look at it. He had permission to bring it home, though it may be from an ancient culture who worshipped evil spirits. He was honest and planned to return it. How is this a clue about what happened to him? Or what brought the lights down in the garage? Is the Wari item related to what happened years ago to Mercedes?"

Lois' tone was soothing when she said, "Oh, Jansen, these are just puzzle pieces, not the answer. Don't you see? We have a clue now about what Doran's deadline is for, and perhaps we can arrange for someone to come here to get the item they want. Without Quincy's background, we'd still be scratching our heads. The rest of the pieces may fall into place soon. Or we may never know this side of heaven what on earth is going on."

Chapter 9

Mary Lou came back to Lois' house, where they planned to read her brother's journal from his backpack. Zeke would stay overnight at Quincy's cottage, but they gathered at Mercedes' place to eat a late dinner.

While she pulled together large salads, baked potatoes, and toasted bread cubes for gluten-free croutons, the two young men sat on the sofa and looked over the photos Jansen had taken. Zeke kept his injured leg propped on a pillow on the sofa table.

Mercedes was uncertain if she wanted to see the paintings. Better, she thought, to get a preview by hearing what her brother and Quincy said about them. So, she pretended to be focused solely on dinner preparations, but she kept an ear to their conversation.

The men believed the paintings Doran had covered were of places said to be portals to other worlds. Some were depicted as caves; others were faux doors into rock, or empty lintels with carvings on them. Doran did not sign these paintings on the front, but on the bottom of the canvas-wrapped wooden stretcher bars.

Her brother shot a glance toward the kitchen. "Hey, Mercedes, you once told me you never sign your paintings until you're finished and certain you won't be embarrassed for anyone to know you did them. Are there any circumstances where you'd sign them out of sight on the bottom?"

She paused from scooping homemade chicken salad onto lettuce. "Yes, if my identity would distract from the purpose of the painting. Like, if the work was for book illustrations, brochures, museum displays—things like that. Unless the buyer specified where my signature was to go, I'd sign on the canvas stapled along the back stretcher bar of the painting. I'd include, along with the title, year completed, maybe the longitude and latitude, and other important facts. It would be easier for the collector to find. But Doran's signature would be closer to the painting if the canvas was ever taken off the stretcher bars to be rolled up."

"Ah, makes sense," Zeke said. "These aren't the views you hang in your living room, so he was working for someone. Doran used longitude and latitude in his line of work—why didn't he record that on the paintings?"

Quincy leaned closer and pointed to another photo. "What do you make of this emblem on the back? Something about it is familiar."

Mercedes placed her dinner on the table while the men zoomed in the photos, trying to decipher the details of the emblem. "Guys, I'm starving. I'll bring your plates on a tray, so you don't have to limp over here, if you let me know whenever you're ready to eat."

Zeke set the cellphone down. "No, we should get away from this a little while. I'll make it to the table with the cane."

"Okay, wash up at the sink," said Mercedes. While she pulled their plates from the refrigerator, they heard a notification for a text message on Zeke's phone.

"I'll get your phone. You get to the table without falling," Quincy said, and he stood up stiffly. "Bless the food, so Mercedes and I can eat."

When they sat down, Zeke checked his phone. He groaned and looked at Mercedes. She shot back a knowing look. "It's Mom or Dad, right? How many times did they check on you today?"

"Three," he answered, buttering his baked potato. "Dad, then Mom a couple hours later, and how could I explain what happened over a text? So, I just said we were okay, and I'd catch them up tonight. Did they try your phone?"

Mercedes swallowed a bite of her salad. "Yes, but only once, and I legitimately told Mom I was busy working with Aaron on evaluating the house. This was before you got hurt in the studio, so there was nothing to report. What is your new text about?"

He picked his phone up again, then he sighed. "They didn't buy it. The rescue operation is underway. They should be here before noon tomorrow."

"Dad expected something would happen," Mercedes said. "He acted strange about you coming here. When he's like this, you can't put him off."

"Will it satisfy him if I just tell him what happened this afternoon?"

After a sip of water, Mercedes shook her head. "No. He believed me in Peru, and he senses the same thing is happening again. You'll be confirming what he knows. Mary Lou's house is dangerous for us."

She looked at Quincy. "For all three of us—and he's my father, considered by the enemy to be my head of the family until I marry. The entity's threat to me was to quit my calling in the Ellison bloodline. Dad's coming because he knows how to confront the enemy, and I'm guessing he'll bring Grandpa."

They ate in silence. Several times, Zeke looked up at Quincy across the table, but his friend silently focused on eating dinner. Finally, Zeke set down his fork and said, "When I came here this morning, I didn't have a grip on what was going on. Until Mercedes told me what happened at the dig site, showed me the journal entry, and I went personally to the Marlowe house, I couldn't have perceived how much it all added to that morning that Mary Lou screamed for help."

He settled back in his chair and watched Quincy. "What are you going to tell your dad, Quincy? Did he try to contact you today?"

Quincy swallowed the last bite of his salad and looked at Mercedes. "I don't know if I was starving for something this healthy to eat after so long on the dig in St. Augustine, or if the takeout lunch today wasn't what I needed. But the dinner was splendid, and I appreciate all the work you put into it. Thank you."

She smiled and said it was her pleasure, and his smile was quick as he reached out to take her hand. Then he looked across the table at Zeke. "Before I came over this morning, I surprised my dad by telling him the report on the dig in Peru wasn't the way I remembered it. I asked for the original records and photos, and he said he and your dad tidied it up to only reflect what the sponsor hired them to find. It shook him up that Doran Marlowe had an artifact linked to that area and that Mercedes was among those who found him dead. And before I left, he made a strange request. He asked me to be wary and alert, just as if I'm on a dig site."

They sat silently, considering this new angle. Mercedes inclined her head to the living room area. "Let's go sit down."

The men cleared the table while Mercedes went to sit on the sofa, and they made quick work of loading the dishwasher before they joined her. Late evening sun rays filtered through the trees around the pool and shone through the glass French doors, setting the room aglow with the moments it had until twilight.

Quincy sat beside Mercedes, as he had that morning before he stormed out. Zeke took the same chair across from them. "My dad did text me again this afternoon, reminding me he was waiting to talk when I get home tonight. I'm not sure what I'll say because I don't know what to expect from him. If you don't mind leaving soon, we'll walk to my cottage, because I want this to be a speaker call between the three of us guys."

Zeke raised his brows and studied Quincy. Then he nodded and turned to Mercedes. "You'll be okay here alone? I'll call mom and dad for us."

"I'm tired and want a shower. My mind is racing with so many possibilities of that Wari artifact and what Doran Marlowe was working on, but I plan to go to bed soon and try to sleep. If I get spooked, I'll go over to spend time with Lois and Mary Lou. I'd love to read Doran's journal."

Mercedes waved while they went out the door into the haunting colors of a Lowcountry twilight. She reminded her brother to send her love to their parents. Then she turned away sadly.

There had been no special goodbye or goodnight from Quincy as he left with Zeke. He had changed since his outburst of anger that morning, when he learned she had kept a secret from him. How would this affect their relationship? His detachment was no way to enter a marriage.

What would happen when her father arrived tomorrow? He would notice the estrangement between them, and Zeke would tell him tonight that she broke her agreement with Quincy's father, Jonathan Holmwood, because of the situation she and Quincy were facing today. Though she was uncertain if this would damage her relationship with her future father-in-law, the passage from the past in her Great-Great Grand Aunt's journal removed all doubt that she must tell Quincy the truth about what happened.

Though Jonathan Holmwood's family had long been friends with the Ellisons, he had revealed his true feelings about what he thought of the unusual things that popped up in her life. If her father took in the situation at the Marlowe house tomorrow, it would deepen her identity as an Ellison, with all the traits that made Jonathan so uncomfortable. It would also remind him he had brushed aside any importance about what happened to her on his dig site, and now it had become unfinished business linked to his son. Would this chill the relationship between the families and end her engagement with Quincy?

She rubbed her hands over her face and breathed a prayer for them all as she wearily headed to the shower.

Mercedes was in her pajamas and getting into bed when her phone chimed with a text. Hoping it was Quincy, she checked the message and sighed.

It was Jana. *Can I call for a few minutes? Sorry it's late, but we just got home from having dinner with Zach.*

Plopping down on her bed in surprise, Mercedes' heart jumped at Zach's name. It seemed so long ago that she had come to this cottage for the summer and planned to meet him while he was here for a retreat with his new company.

Then he had deserted her without even checking to see if she was okay after his new boss tried to murder her, saying she had ruined his life and he never wanted to see her again. Weeks later, he tried to save her and almost got himself killed. What does a woman do with someone like that from her past?

Mercedes hesitated. She had enough trouble right now and her mind couldn't handle more.

She almost yelped when her phone rang in her hands. On the second ring, she decided not to ignore her friend. "Hi, Jana."

"Hey Mercedes, I'm sorry to call so late, but you haven't gotten in touch with me for a couple of days since that emergency you mentioned. And I just felt I needed to tell you something. Are you alone?"

Settling into bed, Mercedes plumped her pillow to lean back on. "Yeah, I'm exhausted and getting into bed. Can we arrange lunch together so I can tell you about that emergency? In the meantime, I'm smack in the middle of another mess and can use some prayers."

"About the situation? Or about handling the wedding with Quincy's family?"

Mercedes tried to think back to what she told Jana about the wedding the morning when Mary Lou screamed from her porch. "Oh. Certainly, for the situation. It's complicated, but I know the woman who was screaming. Now, my parents are involved and coming down tomorrow. And, well, Quincy and

I have bumped into a messy situation, as well. I don't know what's going to happen."

Jana was quiet, then said slowly, "That's a lot to take in, Mercedes. Little wonder you need prayer."

Bursting out in a nervous laugh, Mercedes let it release her tension. Tears sprang up, and she sniffed as she wiped them away.

"Mercedes, are you okay? Honestly?"

"I'm so confused right now, I can't say so with any conviction. But I know I'll be better after I get some sleep. It was a strange day and tomorrow will be even stranger."

"I wonder if I should bring up what I wanted to tell you," Jana said. "It seems so unimportant now."

"Go ahead, you've got me as long as I can stay awake."

"This isn't likely to put you to sleep. Declan and I had dinner out tonight with Zach. He's made a lot of progress and way ahead of his treatment schedule, so Jesus is answering our prayers for his recovery. He looks great and Declan picks on him about a cute rehab therapist who's trying to turn his head. But Zach, you know how he is. He's only amused at her attention."

"Oh, Jana, that's great news! About his recovery, I mean. It's just like him to exceed all expectations. The guy is driven."

Jana's tone turned sad. "He's also in love with you, Mercedes. Anyone who pays attention and knows him can see it. The way he tries to hide how he feels is exactly what gives him away. He asked how you were doing these days, and when I told you cut off our last call to go rescue a screaming woman, he almost spat out his drink of water laughing. He said, 'Oh yeah? Well, now we keep an eye on the news, and she'll turn up as part of a bizarre investigation with a sketchy police report.'"

An unexpected stab at the truth of Zach Boone's statement ripped through her heart. He had been in the last sketchy police report. Unsettled, she sighed.

In a sober tone, Jana said, "That's what's happening, isn't it, Mercedes? That's why you need my prayers?"

Mercedes whispered, "Yes. But it's so much more than that. A man is dead under mysterious circumstances."

"Oh, my. This sounds serious and I know there's much more to this story. I'm glad your family is coming down there. And I can hardly wait until we have lunch so I can hear about it. Listen, before I let you go, I just wanted to tell you that Zach said maybe someday you'll be looking for an excellent attorney, and if you do, he hopes you'll remember him. It sounds like he overruled the warning his parents sent for you never to contact him again."

Mercedes was making tea and cutting up an apple when someone knocked on her door the next morning. She opened it to see Lois and Mary Lou, and she quickly invited them in.

"Can I get you two anything? I just made some lemon tea and I have some fresh blueberry muffins," she asked.

"Sounds marvelous!" said Mary Lou. "But I only have room for tea. Lois made a big breakfast, and we just finished."

"Make that two," Lois said. "I hope we aren't keeping you from anything."

Mercedes smiled and waved a hand toward the open living room area. "Nothing at all, so find a comfortable seat and I'll bring the tea. Why don't you show Mary Lou what you did with this cottage?"

When the ladies gathered in comfortable chairs with their teacups, Lois and Mary Lou told Mercedes about the time they spent reading Doran's journal. They kept a list of noteworthy things and dates that might shed light on what Doran was working on and who he was working with.

Mary Lou took the list from her purse and handed it to Mercedes. "I think some of this will help, but I wanted to tell you that Lois and I also found evidence for all that really matters to me."

Mercedes' hope-filled eyes darted up to Mary Lou's face. "About Doran's salvation?" she asked in hushed excitement.

Lois and Mary Lou exchanged looks, smiling, and Mary Lou suddenly had to brush away a tear. "Yes," she said shakily, pulling a tissue from her bag.

They waited for her to recover and clear her throat. "Throughout the journal ran a theme that tells me he sincerely believed in the Jesus of the Bible, not one he fashioned for himself from all the religious practices he saw over his years traveling."

"He often mentioned Jesus as the Creator," Lois said. "In several places he traveled before retiring, he described the views he was looking at and how moved he was at the Lord's handiwork. Doran had learned so much about the reality of evil's presence in this world and it amazed him how the Lord faithfully and continually proved His existence despite the darkness."

"Oh," breathed Mercedes. "Mary Lou, this is so encouraging. You may compose these things into a testimony of sorts for when you're ready to speak to the media about his life and death. Most who followed him were likely looking for the history and adventure of his travels, and they need to hear about his Christian faith."

"I believe that was on his mind when he agreed to work with an independent film organization who was combining his work with several other explorers and scholars. According to his journal, he was hesitant to do the project at first. He became a consultant, then a contributor, to the documentary," said Mary Lou. She inclined her head to the note in Mercedes' hand. "I jotted down the contact for the organization on the list you have."

Mercedes eagerly looked at the information. Lois said, "Doran wrote a couple of sentences one day to say that he got over his wariness of the project once he saw the producer wanted to present the information from a Biblical framework rather than an evolutionary one. They commissioned him to create a series of paintings for the documentary when the producer thought it would be good to combine Doran's skill as a painter with ritual traditions handed down to local tribes over the generations."

"But a few recent notes he jotted down show that he came to regret it," Mary Lou added. "He was cryptic, but I know how he writes and thinks. He jotted down a note about finishing an occult themed series and he dreaded the time in the studio. But he had a deadline. He doesn't say if the deadline is for the film, or to deliver that artifact in the letter in his backpack."

Mercedes looked up from the list. "Mary Lou, did you try to get into Doran's phone? The answer may be there."

Mary Lou and Lois looked quickly at each other. Mary Lou swatted a hand at her forehead and said, "We were so intrigued with the journal that we forgot about the phone."

She reached for her purse again and unzipped a pocket. "I'm afraid I'm of no help. I don't even know how to turn it on."

Lois took the phone and looked it over, then tried one button. "We will need a password to verify that we're allowed to open this."

Seeing Mary Lou's blank look, Mercedes rose to go get a notepad. "Let's brainstorm a few ideas."

"It's turning on. I'll try the numbers for Mary Lou's name while you get something to write on."

Mercedes was back before Lois got the digits entered and the phone said the password was incorrect. She jotted down 4 options and handed the notepad to Lois. "That was a great guess, to use his sister's name. Try these."

The second option opened the phone. Lois gasped. The phone sounded with several notifications, and Mercedes reached for the pad to circle the Bible verse reference to show which one worked. "Mary Lou, I don't want to sound bossy. I'm just trying to help. But you need to memorize this password. You can write it down on your calendar or somewhere easy to see, but don't write that it's a password and don't keep it with the phone. Have Lois hold on to a list of passwords at her house in case of an emergency."

She held Mary Lou's eyes. "If anything happens to you and you cannot respond to health care workers, it will be important for friends to have a record of things like this."

Mary Lou nodded and said quietly, "I know you're trying to help me, and I need it so much. Doran—he planned for a will with our attorney, but not for other practical things. I'm sure he thought that in a few weeks, we'd get the remodeling project underway, and he would teach me how to manage things like the finances, passwords, and to practice driving again."

Mercedes smiled comfortingly at her. "Of course. But this didn't take Jesus by surprise. Our culture is a shock from what you've been used to, and the Lord provided help in Doran's absence. You are not bothering us, so please ask if you need anything."

"I'm still stunned that you guessed the right password for Doran's phone," Lois said, shaking her head as she explored the screen. "How did you do it?"

Shrugging, Mercedes winked at Mary Lou. "His sister's happiness. Mary Lou, what point do you have to start with in the mission field to establish that Jesus is not just a god among gods?"

"Oh. That He is the Creator God, the one above all, the one who rules over all. No other god is like Him, and no other god is before Him."

"And I noticed that point convinced you that your brother had salvation in Jesus. You said it came across as a theme through his journal. So, I chose a verse about how He created the world before anything else existed. We could have tried different combinations, but the second one worked. Doran kept it simple."

Lois searched the screen for phone calls and messages. "I have a text message here from the man mentioned with the independent film organization," she announced. "It looks like a couple of calls are from the same number."

"Mary Lou, if you're comfortable with this suggestion, let's ask my brother and Quincy to come over and handle this contact for us. Quincy has some connections like this organization and can help us learn how to move forward."

"Yes, of course," Mary Lou said. "I'm so relieved! I need to clear up Doran's affairs. If they will check with this person and let him know what has happened to my brother, and ask what we should do with the paintings, it will help me so much."

The women left Zeke and Quincy in the living room at the Marlowe house with Doran's phone and the list of important clues from his journal. The information filled in more of the puzzle for everyone, and if there was a looming deadline they could help to meet, they wanted to help.

Mary Lou, Lois, and Mercedes were close by, working to find any more clues or unpaid bills in Doran's room. Mary Lou was overjoyed to find his Bible in a nightstand.

Mary Lou's boarding house guests would return over the next few days, and Mercedes was concerned. Time was running out to free the house of the menacing presence in the dark passage. She wondered when her parents would arrive, and what would come next.

Lois explained an insurance policy from the filing cabinet to Mary Lou when someone knocked briskly on the front door, then pushed it open a bit and saw Zeke and Quincy. Aaron's lazy drawl greeted them as he stepped in and closed the door behind him. He listened to the progress the men were making, then came to Doran's open door to pop his head in.

Mercedes grinned as she looked for the special exchange that always passed between Lois and Aaron's eyes when they met. Not for the first time, she wondered why they were not married. Both were retired, both were widows, both had an adult child who lived on their own, and Lois had a young adult granddaughter. Quincy and Mercedes occasionally shared date nights with them. But they weren't the only friends she had who enjoyed being couples only for companionship, not romance.

Aaron added a wink to his special look with Lois today. Smiling, he said, "Ladies, a storm is supposed to move in and leave us with the gift of a cooler, beautiful evening. You're all invited to a fish fry and grill later at Lois' house. My buddies had a big haul today, and it's more than they can sell. I'll make up some coleslaw and roasted potatoes and onions. It sounds like we're havin' some out-of-town guests, so we want to feed them well."

"My mouth is already watering, Aaron, and I know my family will love it!" Mercedes said. "Let me know how I can help after we're done here."

They all turned as another visitor arrived, ringing the doorbell rather than knocking. Aaron made his way to greet another guest.

The thickly accented voice was indistinct, but Mary Lou's head jerked up and she gasped. Mercedes knew this was John, the friend who kept coming to Mary Lou's mind from the mission field.

Aaron ushered the visitor in while Mary Lou rushed from Doran's room to go greet him. "John!" she exclaimed, then put her hands to her mouth in disbelief as she stopped to stare at the swarthy-complexioned man who held a beige broad-brimmed hat in his hands.

Mercedes came into the foyer in time to witness their reunion, and she knew in an instant that she was right about his identity. He fit the description that Jansen Kirk and the law enforcement officer had given them two days before, and he and Mary Lou clearly were overjoyed to see one another.

When they parted from the bear hugs, Mary Lou marveled at how John was so grown up and such a man now, while she had only gotten shriveled and older. But love and admiration filled his eyes when he shook his head and grinned. "Lulu, you are still so beautiful. You are the reason I came to America, with the mission board, to learn more and to visit the woman who shared the message of salvation in Jesus to my people. Our church there is growing, and most of the people have turned away from the old gods."

Mary Lou searched his face in disbelief, and Aaron said, "I think you and Mary Lou have a lot to catch up on. Let's sit down."

"Here, sit together on the sofa," Zeke said, gathering his notes from the coffee table and handing them to Quincy before taking Doran's old cane to move to another chair. "Quincy and I have done all we can right now."

"Can I bring you something to drink, John?" offered Lois. She took a few steps toward the kitchen.

Mercedes held her breath as she watched John's face change. He still held Mary Lou's hand as he stared alertly down the short hallway that connected the kitchen to the living room. She and Mary Lou followed his eyes to the cross that hung on the door that led to the dark passage and Doran's studio.

Lois stood still, and everyone waited. Finally, John said, "Lulu, I know a thing. I can help."

Mary Lou's answer came in a hoarse whisper. "Did you know before you traveled here? Have you been thinking of what you would say, how you could tell me what you need to do?"

He turned to look deeply into her eyes. "Yes, Lulu, and I prayed often. I know this thing, and I know what to do. You have great sorrow in your heart. But I am here now, and you will be safe."

With a nod toward the passage door, he said, "This is the same cross I remember. You kept it wherever you dwelt with us, in my village." Then John glanced around at the rest of the group before he started speaking to Mary Lou in his own language.

Mary Lou turned to them and said, "John must switch to speaking and thinking in his native language. And he's asking me some questions about my friends. I'll translate when he wants me to."

Another knock on the front door behind them made them start, and Aaron looked at Mary Lou for permission to answer it. She looked at John, and they exchanged words Mercedes did not understand.

"It's okay. Open the door, please, Aaron," she said in English.

Mercedes heard her grandfather introduce himself and saw Aaron reach out to shake hands with him and her father. Relief washed over her, and her eyes searched the room to find her brother's.

Zeke and Quincy had risen to their feet expectantly, and Zeke gave her a wink. Mary Lou and John exchanged more conversations in his language, and Mercedes could understand bits of it. He mentioned her family's last name.

Mary Lou said, "John says we need to leave our cellphones here and follow him outside to join the Ellison family. Lois, Aaron, and Quincy may join us, but the Ellisons are to stand with him."

Mercedes' hand went to her mouth. Wide-eyed, she looked for Zeke, who was already making his way to her. He barely used the cane, so she knew he was much better, but it was still evidence of what happened yesterday.

And only heaven knew what might happen now.

Chapter 10

"The best kiss is the one that has been exchanged a thousand times between the eyes before it reaches the lips." Unknown

While Mercedes' family and friends gathered outside, Mary Lou took John into the garage studio and told him about the angry buzzing sound they heard before the lights started falling over the spot where Zeke, Quincy, and Mercedes had been standing in front of Doran's painting. John threw back the covers on Doran's paintings to see them, then he left the studio.

He told Mary Lou to leave the door to the garage open. Then he asked for her keys, and he unlocked the door to the shuttered passage. Mercedes breathlessly waited to see what would happen, remembering how this door repelled her on the day she found Doran's body.

John hesitated for only a moment, then turned the knob. It resisted at first, swollen from humidity, but he finally pulled it free and let it swing open.

Nothing happened. Mercedes wondered if the presence she knew to be around was in there or had remained in the garage studio. It was not attacking John, who turned his back and came to the group.

Ominous clouds filled the darkening sky and leaves trembled in the gusty breezes. Gusts of soggy wind pushed at Mercedes' hair, and she regretted not having anything to pull it into a ponytail with. She turned her head so it would blow away from her face. Jansen jogged up to Zeke and Quincy, asking them what was happening and if the man with them was Mary Lou's friend.

John's loose fitting white shirt tugged at its buttons in sudden wind gusts, and Mercedes thought he looked formidable standing there in Mary Lou's yard. He locked eyes with Jansen and said in English, "Do you believe now?"

The young doctor swallowed hard, nodded, and answered, "Yes, I believe. I don't understand, but I want to be part of this."

Thunder rumbled overhead. John said, "Stand with your friends and do not falter."

Jansen swallowed hard, staring at John. Quickly, Quincy drew him into the circle of friends gathered in front of the passageway. Everyone grasped hands together in a circle as lightning threatened from a distance. Mercedes wondered if anyone else felt the surge of energy from under their feet. Adrenaline swelled in her and she tried to steady her breathing.

Beside her, her father held her hand. Her mother was next, then her grandparents. John was next to her grandfather, and she saw him look down at the grass and crushed shell gravel under his black athletic shoes. Mary Lou gripped his other hand and looked down in surprise.

They felt it! She was not the only one, not the weird one, not the one whose imagination ran away with her. Long blonde strands of hair whipped across her face and again she tossed her head, turning to see her brother beside her and Quincy beside him.

Quincy's blue eyes were alert, watching the ground under his shoes with curiosity, but no hint of fear. The wind gusts tossed his dark hair and his shirt rippled like waves in a strong sea breeze, but his tanned face was a study in concentration.

She saw Jansen look from him to Zeke with expectation, as if they had the answers he wanted to ask for. Then she heard John speaking in his native language again and turned to watch his face.

Mary Lou spoke up over the wind and low rumble of distant thunder. "John says, we are here because we all agree that there is a presence in this dark passage that has left its territory and must return. Pray with him when he uses English and then repeat those words when we don't understand him any longer. He will use an ancient tongue from his village that is not for us."

As John started praying, everyone in the group joined in. At first, they watched him, but soon they followed his eyes to the open door of what they now thought of as the dark passage.

Mercedes felt a rush of danger that swept her breath away, but a surge of confidence and focus pushed it aside. John's voice never wavered, and his purpose was clear as he led them in prayer. They repeated his declarations of how there was a name above all names, a king above all kings, who defeated death when his spiritual enemies thought they had killed him and set themselves free.

"His name is Jesus!" proclaimed John, and as he raised his clasped hands with Mary Lou and Deacon, Mercedes' grandfather, lightning reflected in a flash of light from the silver of his wristwatch. Mercedes' heart overflowed with love and a sense of awe as she and the others repeated the name of their Savior several times, and she wondered if it was thunder that rattled the windows in the dark passage.

John led them to praise Jesus for His power over evil and they consecrated and dedicated Mary Lou's house for Jesus' glory, asking that He open its doors to be a sanctuary, ready with opportunities to share the Gospel message of salvation.

The drizzle of cool rain mingled with Mary Lou and Lois' tears as John slipped into words they no longer understood. Beside him, Mercedes' grandfather led them in the praises they followed with John. They declared Jesus as the name above all names, the power over all powers, and the owner and ruler over Mary Lou's house.

Many things happened all at once. A blast of wind hit Mercedes so hard that it was only her hands clasped firmly with her father and brother that kept her on her feet. Both moved in a bit as a shield in front of her. John, Mary Lou, and Mercedes' grandfather swayed and almost staggered, as did several others in the group. But they remained steadfast on their feet while the door to the dark passage banged on its hinges. A crashing sound in the passage competed with the clap of thunder and the peal of lightning that startled residents in Bluffton, South Carolina and made the dishes in their cabinets rattle.

Suddenly, sunrays peeked in and out while the black clouds raced away. The group stood, speechless, heady with the victory they sensed had freed Mary Lou's house and become a landmark of each person's faith to look back on.

John led the group in a prayer of praise, thanking Jesus for the victory He had won and for the privilege of letting them join Him in His work. Then, he let go of the hands of those beside him and declared that Jesus reigned in Mary Lou's house.

Tears stood in Mercedes' eyes as she turned to her parents, hugging them with joy. Then her grandparents' arms enveloped her, and she knew she was right where Jesus wanted her to be.

She was an Ellison of the once-legendary Ellisons, and she had stopped running from her calling. There was no shame in fighting spiritual battles in invisible places.

Quincy turned from Zeke and Jansen to find Mercedes. He pulled her close in exhilaration and relief from what they had just been part of, but words failed him.

Opening his eyes again, he saw his parents walking across the street to join them. His eyes met his mother's, and her smile was tremulous. He knew they had witnessed what had happened.

His dad's face was impassive, as if nothing unusual had occurred. Mercedes' mom and grandmother turned to welcome them and introduce them to the others.

"We told Quincy we were coming to visit him this afternoon, but when we found he wasn't at his cottage, we knew he might be here," Tiffany Holmwood said. "We parked across the street at the playground to walk over, then the storm caught us unaware."

She turned to hug Quincy and whisper that she was glad he was all right. Jonathan said, "We got to the corner when everyone was gathering, and we didn't want to interrupt." His eyes roamed from Quincy to the open passage door. "So, we waited."

Mercedes turned to John, who nodded and stepped toward the door. "There is nothing to fear. I will look for that which brought trouble."

She took Quincy's hand and smiled. "A dig site isn't the only place to find artifacts," she said. "Take your father and go see what Doran brought home."

The passage was no longer so dark. But it was a wreck.

Shelves had fallen, and anything that was not in crates had crashed to the floor or onto boxes. Mercedes peeked in while Zeke, Quincy, Jansen, and Jonathan followed John, who scanned the fallen objects. Presently, he squatted and picked up an item that had broken into three pieces.

He murmured something in his language and turned to the others. "If you see an empty box, will you please pass it to me?"

Jonathan was the first to find one. John laid what looked like a statue with a grotesque face in the bottom, then looked around again. "It's getting late. You may search for what is on the floor. The other boxes can wait until tomorrow."

From the doorway, Mercedes asked, "John, can you share what you were saying in your language while we prayed outside? I only recognized a few words."

He turned gentle brown eyes to hers and seemed to consider his answer. "Some words were from another age. Jesus empowered the words to overcome the evil spirit in the painting. There were other, lesser spirits in this room, among these things. They are gone now, and all this must go. These have no place in a house where Jesus rules."

She nodded. "I understand. Something in here was associated with a certain spirit that I encountered in your country. Did you find it?"

"Yes, it is in the box. It is only stone now. I will destroy it."

Jansen glanced at her, then at John. "It's only stone now? Then what was it before?"

"Stonework idols are not just craftsmanship," John answered, looking at the fragments of another carved image and tossing them in the same box. "The people who worshipped these held many rituals over them. They are not spiritually neutral."

"When you get home, search online for a process called the 'opening of the mouth ceremony,'" Zeke added, picking up a broken earthenware pot with symbols painted on it. "I can text you some other creepy leads, too."

"My father, he was a shaman," said John, picking up another broken item and studying it. He tossed it into the box, where it hit another stone and cracked. "I know many things. I have seen the works of many gods. But Jesus saved me, and he came to me and my mother in our dreams. Then the missionaries came to teach us the Bible. My father was furious and said I was no son of his. Lulu's missionaries took me in."

He stopped and turned to look at them. "I know about the god that came to this house. Lulu's brother did not understand. He thought it was a carving, with no life in it. The god tricked him into bringing it here. But Jesus, He knew what He would do. He let the being deceive her brother and leave its territory in search of the young Ellison woman. Today, Jesus sent the spirit back. Do not be afraid. It is no threat to you here."

The setting sun gleamed on Lois' windows. Around the pool and courtyard, the freshness of an evening after a storm embraced her guests. The shadows stretched long and mysterious in distorted shapes on the pavers.

Aaron cleaned the remnants of fish off the grill, and Mary Lou carried an empty dessert tray into the house. She would spend the night here again with Lois while John stayed at her house. One of the first things she noticed after the chaos in the dark passage that afternoon was the smell of decay was no longer present in the main house. She hoped to stash her air filter away.

Tomorrow, her boarding guests were due to return home. They would learn that Doran had died unexpectedly of a heart attack and Mary Lou set his funeral for the next week. And they would meet John, who planned to stay to help Mary Lou until he finished online training with the Mission Board. They were going to tear down the passage and build a spacious sunroom to connect the garage and the house.

As Mercedes helped Lois by spreading cling wrap over some leftovers, she heard Zeke and Quincy explain to their parents that Doran was working with an independent filmmaker on a documentary about his travels. His contact was stunned at Doran's passing and changed his schedule to fly into Hilton Head the next day.

Zeke said, "Quincy and I are going to take tomorrow off to meet him and help him gather whatever he and Doran were planning to use. This may change the direction of the documentary and put it in the status of a memorial tribute, but the producer promised to bring a contract that Mary Lou can sign in Doran's place if she wants to carry on with it. The paintings have the film company's logo on the back, so he designated them for the documentary."

"I'm expected in St. Augustine the next day, though," said Quincy. "As much as I'd like to stay and help sort through Doran's collection in the passage, I have a contract. Someone else must contact museums for the donations."

Jonathan Holmwood leaned forward. "I'll help tie up loose ends here for you, Quincy." He looked over at his wife. "Tiffany and I drove separate cars so she can return to help my parents. I'll extend my room reservation and see if I can catalog anything for Doran's sister. I'm also willing to meet the deadline to deliver the item he's supposed to return to the authorities in Peru. The right people probably remember me."

"I can stay," offered Dawson Ellison. He turned to his wife, and she smiled and nodded her approval. "Josette, I'll leave it up to you if you want to spend a few days here visiting Lois and getting in some shopping with Mercedes."

Mercedes finished covering the food and handed a laden tray to Lois, who was on her way to the back door that led to the kitchen. She pulled up a chair between her brother and Quincy, who made room for her to come closer to the group, and Quincy loosely took her hand.

"So, which one of you talked to Jansen Kirk last night?" she asked. "It surprised me when John asked him if he believes, and I know it wasn't about Santa Claus."

Zeke and Quincy laughed outright and exchanged conspiratorial glances while chuckles spread around the patio table. "I called him with thanks for the photos of the paintings in Doran's studio," Zeke said. "You know how curious he is. He asked about what I was thinking of them. I put him on speaker and Quincy could share his thoughts, too."

He leaned in to look at Quincy. "I don't remember how we got from that topic to him accepting salvation in Jesus, do you?"

Quincy shook his head. "Now that you mention it, no. But you guys shared some miraculous things you'd seen with patients, and what made Biblical Christianity stand out from any other religion. I think you got him with the point that it's the only belief system whose Savior is alive and doesn't require us to earn our way to heaven."

"Yeah!" Zeke exclaimed, slapping his hand on his thigh and looking at Mercedes. "That's it, Quincy's right. Jansen had never compared what other religions believe before. To be honest, Jesus was working hard on him, and he asked me right there how to pray. I'm sure that whatever all this was about, there was no coincidence when Dr. Jansen Kirk arrived to help you with Mary Lou when she found her brother in his studio."

Zeke's grandmother had tears standing in her eyes, which she wiped away with her unused dessert napkin and sniffed. "Zekie, I'm so thankful to have been here to hear this story. Both my grandchildren know that being a discerning Christian is often a lonely road."

Under the table, Mercedes lightly slapped the back of her fingers on her brother's leg and tried not to smirk when her grandmother used her nickname for him. She called him Zekie from the day he was born.

Their grandfather smiled and reached for her hand, then turned to Zeke and Mercedes. "And we feel immeasurably blessed to have been part of what happened at the Marlowe house today. It's been a while since we've been so energized, facing a battle like that one. And it's so encouraging, as well—John, Jansen, Zekie, Quincy, and Mercedes, young and strong, standing there, planted with deep roots against the evil that threatened them—if it's the last battle I'm allowed to see, it was the best."

Mercedes stood beside Quincy's sports car as he finished loading up and prepared to drive back to the excavation site at St. Augustine, Florida. "So, when did you say your next job starts?" he asked.

"In two days. It should be an easy one, for a change," she said with a grin.

Quincy looked at her sideways and smirked. "You say that every time."

"And I mean it, every time! In my preliminary work, I see no hauntings, murders, scoundrels, or occult activities associated with the house or the owner. My client is a mother who's giving her daughter a family home in Beaufort."

He situated a box in the back seat in a slot that was just the right size. Then he stood up straight, stretched his injured shoulder, and leaned back on the car. "Did you enjoy shopping with your mom?"

"Oh, yes. The best part is, she always beats me to the cash register. That's especially important when we shop at boutiques on the island."

"What did you buy?"

"Oh, a few things that will blend into a warm autumn around here. Capris in darker colors, a couple of island-vibe tops, a fresh straw handbag with a sunflower on it, and a pair of neutral-colored sandals. I'll wear them next week in Beaufort."

He sighed and rubbed a hand over his forehead, avoiding the lump that was almost gone after the incident in Doran's studio. "I miss the days when I was working here, and we did more together. I never should have taken that job in St. Augustine without setting a firm end date. But at least we got most everything settled for Mary Lou yesterday, and you've got what you need to wrap up the paperwork for her house."

Mercedes looked down at the toe of her flip flop while she absently pushed a wayward seashell from the paver driveway. "Yes, I plan to finish it tonight and go over it with her tomorrow. I'm glad John can stay and study remotely for his role in being a Bible translator. And your dad was a lot of help smoothing over the fact that the statue Doran was returning to the antiquities people was broken."

She looked up and saw herself reflected in his sunglasses for a few moments before he pulled them up on his head. They looked at one another awkwardly, and her heart missed a beat as she got lost in his intense blue gaze. But she did not let herself say something—anything—to cover the fact that things were not the same.

Finally, she looked down at the engagement ring on her left hand, but instantly, he snatched that hand away. "Nothing has changed," he said huskily.

Her eyes stung with tears that a deep breath calmed. "You've changed, Quincy."

A gravelly groan came from his throat, and he glanced away, but then locked eyes with hers again. "Going through changes is a big part of relationships, Mercedes. But my love and loyalty to you have not changed a bit. I don't blame you for what happened with my dad. With much less evidence, I've kept things from you and others on some level over the years, too."

He took her other hand, so now he held both. "What's different now is that you and I never talked about the elephant in the room, about how my dad and grandparents are not thrilled about my decision to spend my life with you. That's my fault. Just be patient with me while I work on them, and if they won't budge, I'll stop trying. Give my dad time to process what he saw at the Marlowe house that day when we all prayed to expel the demon spirit, and to get past the fact that the lights nearly came down on me the day Dawson warned him I could be in danger."

He let her hands go and pulled her to him. Near her ear, he said, "I can't believe you even thought of taking that ring off, Mercedes. I'm so distracted I didn't realize I made you feel like walking away from me."

From nearby, a happy, relentless yap nagged them from a neighbor's window, and Mercedes laughed as she wiped tears away. "Bijou! She sees you packing up and knows what that means. She'll miss you while you're gone."

Quincy sniffed and let her pull back. "Ok, let's go say hello and goodbye to Bijou before I leave."

Seeing that they were going to her front door, the little dog that Mercedes thought looked like a stuffed toy disappeared from the window. But they heard her barking ecstatically as they walked up the porch steps. Before Quincy could ring the bell, his neighbor opened the door so that the tiny dog could try to jump up into Quincy's waiting arms.

"I see you're leaving for work in Florida again," his neighbor said, glowing to see her pet's happiness. "How long will you be away?"

"I'm hoping to be back in a week," Quincy answered, dodging a frantic kiss from Bijou. "I came back for an emergency that Mercedes and Lois were dealing with last week."

The neighbor made a clicking sound of sympathy and touched Mercedes gently on the arm. "I heard about it. I wanted to let all the activity at the house settle down before I stopped in to see Mary Lou. Do you think she'd be okay with me bringing Bijou by for a visit?"

By now, Bijou had wiggled her way into Mercedes' arms, where she calmed down and watched her face with adoration. Mercedes smiled at the sparkling little eyes and lavender glitter bows tied around Bijou's fluffy ears. "Oh, yes," she breathed. "Mary Lou would love a visit from Bijou."

After visiting Bijou, Quincy drove Mercedes to her cottage a few houses away and walked her to the door. He kissed a spot near her ear. "I should've been gone by now. I'll call you after I get there."

"Be careful."

"I will." He walked to his car but stopped and turned before he got there. "Start planning a wedding," he said. "But not at any historical houses. We don't need an unexpected adventure that day."

She was leaning against her door, watching him go, and she grinned. "Okay. For how many guests?"

"I don't know yet."

"Find out. Otherwise, we may hire a pastor and just show up at the gazebo at White Point Gardens one day."

"I like that plan! How about a honeymoon in the Keys? I still dream of the time we spent there."

"I like your plan, too."

"All right. I'll call you in a little while."

"I'll be waiting."

Did you like this novel? You can continue the adventures of Mercedes Ellison in the Strange Sands Series. Remember to help other readers by sharing your review!

There is a list of **Resources** for readers who enjoyed this novella series and want to investigate certain aspects of it. For Book Clubs, there is a page called **Discussion Topics** to help leaders guide conversations and glean more spiritual insight from the stories.

Stay updated with me via my fun-packed author newsletter and websites at Southern Sky Publishing[1] and Pamela Poole Fine Art[2], or join me on YouTube[3], Goodreads[4] and BookBub[5].

1. http://www.southernskypublishing.com

2. http://www.pamelapoole.com

3. https://www.youtube.com/channel/UC9aV3zHRlASXUUBEF7xbT9Q

4. https://www.goodreads.com/author/show/3934732.Pamela_Poole

5. https://www.bookbub.com/profile/pamela-poole

Resources

There are so many! This one is where I find the most helpful research material for both reliable, quick references and for in-depth Bible Study and Biblical Worldview writing.

YouTube has many podcast interviews and conference presentations with the late Dr. Michael S. Heiser about the Bible, but those who want to dig deeper will discover a lot of extra material and primary sources on this scholar's main website. I highly recommend his book *Supernatural* and his videos on the Divine Council and Cosmic Geography:

Dr. Michael S. Heiser[6]

Others:

Alicia Childers (former Zoe Girl singer)
Melissa Dougherty (author of Happy Lies)
Iron and Myth (Derek Gilbert)
Micah Huss (Marginal Mysteries)
The Faull Brothers (Documentaries)
Dr. Judd Burton (archaeology and history)

For Discussion

I interviewed Christian believers about some of their supernatural experiences and have listened to many such stories from the mission field. We should never "educate" ourselves out of believing the realities of the spiritual realm around us and the miracles we see every day. Have you had, or heard of, an experience where an encounter or outcome could only be explained as divine intervention and Providence?

Have you heard missionaries report on the places they serve, and do some of their accounts stick with you over the years? Share these with your reading group.
A church we once belonged to in Charleston, SC, organized a group of our leadership and members, including the pastor and associate pastor, for a mission trip to Cusco, Peru. They came back with a report and a harrowing account of a spiritual attack on them as a group. They huddled in their quarters in a circle and prayed against the evil that surrounded them in an unnerving clamor. Eventually, the enemy they prayed against went away.

When you look around your home, do you see any décor items that could be associated with pagan religions? Are you willing to do some research about the items and find out the beliefs and symbolism attached to them?

About the Author

Inspiring Southern Ambiance

Pamela Poole writes inspirational mystery and suspense that explore the intersection of faith, history, and the unseen spiritual realm. Her stories are grounded in a clear Christian worldview and shaped by a deep respect for both historical preservation and biblical truth.

Pamela writes inspirational stories that bring together Christian faith, historic places, and hidden truths. Her novels reveal how the past can press into the present, where faith becomes essential to discernment and courage. Her characters are ordinary people facing extraordinary challenges, learning to trust Jesus when darkness threatens and answers are not easily found.

Pamela is the author of the Strange Sands Suspense series and the Painter Place Saga, blending richly detailed settings with themes of calling, obedience, redemption, and spiritual warfare. Her fiction offers clean, thought-provoking suspense designed both to engage the imagination and to encourage the heart.

When she isn't writing, Pamela enjoys research, painting in her art studio and on location along the Southern coast and making memories with her family and friends.

Readers and art enthusiasts alike can enjoy her YouTube channel[7] for painting demos and art education presentations. To enjoy the latest content, sign up for her fun-filled newsletters and follow Pamela Poole Fine Art[8] and Southern Sky Publishing[9].

---

7. https://www.youtube.com/channel/UC9aV3zHRlASXUUBEF7xbT9Q

8. https://www.pamelapoole.com/

9. https://www.southernskypublishing.com/

More Books in the Strange Sands Suspense Series

The Old Cedar Chest, Strange Sands Suspense 1
Hilton Head

An antique cedar hope chest.
A hidden document.
A century-spanning vendetta.

The Old Cedar Chest launches a faith-filled suspense novella series following architectural historian Mercedes Annalee Ellison as she uncovers the unexplainable forces tied to historic properties—and her own family legacy.

Mercedes never expected her great-great-grandaunt's fragile journal and a tattered manila envelope to change her life. Yet the miraculous way they came into her possession—and the unease they stir in her spirit—would give even the most hardened skeptic pause.

Before she can meet her first client or settle into what she hopes will be a quiet summer at a Lowcountry cottage, an ominous shadow stretches across her carefully planned future. Mercedes soon realizes she is the target of a vendetta that goes back more than a century. Time is running out, and survival may mean accepting a calling she never sought and a destiny bound to the legendary Ellison family.

In this heart-pounding Christian suspense novella, Mercedes must rely on more than her education and instincts. Anchored in faith and surrounded by eerie revelations, she learns God equips ordinary people to stand firm against extraordinary challenges. Filled with mystery, history, and spiritual depth, The Old Cedar Chest invites readers to consider how faith, courage, and divine purpose intersect in life's unseen battles.

The Hidden Hallway, Strange Sands Suspense 2
Savannah

An antebellum house.
A hidden hallway.
A tale of passion and revenge.

In *The Hidden Hallway*, architectural historian Mercedes Annalee Ellison faces another assignment that challenges not only her professional expertise but her spiritual resolve.

Tammy and Clayton Popplewell hired Mercedes as they registered and renovated an antebellum house in the beautiful Southern city of Savannah, Georgia. But she knows this is not the boring job she hoped for when she arrives on the first day to find the local police there. What should have been a routine assessment of aging blueprints and structural quirks takes a chilling turn when Mercedes uncovers a concealed hallway that doesn't appear on any original plans.

As Mercedes investigates the history of the property, she must rely not only on her expertise but on God's guidance to discern something hidden—and why it matters now. When neighbors seek her out with a strange Civil War Era tale of passion and revenge, she works to uncover a terrifying darkness and help her clients make the house into the inn where they dream of sharing light—before they give up and she loses the job.

The Hidden Hallway is a gripping Christian inspirational suspense novella blending history, mystery, and spiritual warfare. Set against the rich atmosphere of historic Savannah, it's a story of faith tested, dreams endangered, and the assurance that God is always present—especially where secrets hide.

The Freedom Staircase, Strange Sands Suspense 3
Charleston

An enduring Lowcountry plantation.
A legendary patriot refuge.
A last stand for freedom.

It thrilled Mercedes Ellison to be chosen to work as an architectural historian for Majestic Oaks, a plantation that endured and survived wars on American soil. The stately Georgian mansion features the Freedom Staircase, where legendary patriots stopped for refuge in their roles with the Continental Army in the American Revolution. Her client needs help to keep the plantation he inherited, which is steeped in the history of the Lowcountry of South Carolina, home of the Swamp Fox and four signers of the Declaration of Independence.

There are also some unsolved mysteries on the property. Bringing them to light will help her client, and she finds clues in a secret passage used by the patriots. But then her archenemy dies in jail, and his son watches her. The long-standing vendetta against the Ellison family that began in *The Old Cedar Chest* now escalates, and Mercedes knows the danger she faces is real, personal, and relentless. Can she make a last stand for freedom from the past that began with the murder of her ancestor on a stormy night in England?

Blending historical intrigue, Christian faith, and suspense, *The Freedom Staircase* is an inspirational story of legacy, obedience, and the courage to walk the path God sets before us, even when it leads straight through danger.

The Dark Passage, Strange Sands Suspense 4
Bluffton

Faith tested.
Purpose questioned.
Evil revealed.

Mercedes Ellison is hoping for a quiet summer as she plans her
wedding—boring clients, simple renovations, no surprises. But the
Marlowe House is anything but ordinary.
Doran Marlowe, a former missionary guide, has spent decades traveling the
world's most remote regions. His shuttered passageway and unsettling
artwork hint at experiences he never fully left behind. His sister Mary Lou,
newly returned from the mission field, carries her own
burdens—discouragement, doubt, and unanswered questions about her
calling.
When a terrifying incident shatters the calm of the historic home,
Mercedes finds herself drawn into a mystery that defies logic and
explanation. The danger feels personal, spiritual, and disturbingly familiar.
In *The Dark Passage*, Pamela Poole weaves a faith-filled suspense story that
confronts spiritual darkness with biblical truth. This inspirational mystery
asks hard questions about obedience, spiritual authority, and trusting God
when the unseen world breaks into the ordinary.

The Devil's Drawer, Strange Sands Suspense 5
Beaufort

An ominous oath taken for personal privilege.
An enigmatic artifact unbound by time and place.
An evil consequence for generations.

A chilling mystery unfolds at Seashell Cottage as architectural historian Mercedes Ellison stumbles upon an ominous black cabinet decorated with ancient Egyptian symbols. Delivered under the cover of darkness, this enigmatic artifact pulls her and her client into a web of secrets that stretches across generations.

As they delve deeper, a private investigator friend joins them in unraveling the sinister connection between the cabinet and a long-buried family oath to a clandestine society. With blood as the ultimate spiritual currency, they must confront the haunting legacy of a deceased ancestor whose evil choices ripple through time, binding Mercedes' client in ways they never imagined.

This gripping story is filled with suspense, intrigue, and revelations. As a Christian, Mercedes knows that Jesus reverses curses. But will her client come to know this before it is too late?

Grab your copy today and join Mercedes on this thrilling adventure!

Coming in 2026!
The Black Hourglass, Strange Sands Suspense 6
St. Augustine

In the shadow lies the truth.
A hidden letter.
A stolen fortune.
A secret that refused to stay buried.

Quincy Holmwood thought his work in St. Augustine was over until a cryptic message from a church archivist pulled him back into a mystery from 1688. How can he resist a search for the truth left by a murdered friar about hidden evidence of a crime against the Crown, committed by a powerful group of colonial settlers of America's oldest city? The trail of clues had endured for the courageous man of a future generation who was bold enough to follow them.

With his fiancée, **Mercedes Ellison**, and a small archaeology team, Quincy races to decode symbols tied to a forgotten brotherhood whose emblem—the **black hourglass**—marks the flow of time the brotherhood believed was under their control.

The brotherhood's final heir is watching his progress.

And he never wants the past to come to light.

As accidents turn deadly, Quincy must rely on his faith and the conviction that he is the one the friar believed would someday reveal the truth.

What was hidden in darkness was never meant to stay there.

Other Books by Pamela Poole
<u>Southern Sky Publishing</u>[10]

The Painter Place Saga
Painter Place
Hugo
Jaguar
Landmark
3 Legends of Painter Place (short stories)
The Wind Songs of the Marsh
King's Ransom
The Castaway and the Mermaid

Southern Sky Devotional
Inspired Artistry—Embracing the Creative Calling

---

10. https://www.southernskypublishing.com/